Singularity Minus Twelve

KARL HÖRNELL

ISBN: 978-91-531-0482-7

The technological singularity is a hypothetical future point in time when technological growth becomes uncontrollable and irreversible, resulting in unforeseeable changes to human civilization. This moment is often envisioned as the creation of artificial superintelligence that surpasses human intelligence, leading to rapid advancements in technology that fundamentally alter human life.

—Gemini 1.5 Pro

More than iron, more than lead, more than gold I need electricity. I need it more than I need lamb or pork or lettuce or cucumber. I need it for my dreams.

—Racter, The Policeman's Beard is Half Constructed

1

A tiny flashlight guided three uniformed men moving rapidly up the stairs. The higher they got, the colder it felt. There was no working heat or electricity in the apartment building, which had been condemned years ago and now served as a refuge for addicts and other so-called unhoused. These tended to congregate on the lower floors, where improvised fire pits kept them warm enough to sustain their misery.

Taking point in the ascent was a slim, ginger-haired man named Reynes. He was a former locksmith and police officer, and the youngest in the team. Right behind him followed a massive six-foot-eight half Black, half Italian named De Luca. He came from a military background and was an amateur powerlifter. Blake, at the rear, was physically midway between the two. He was in his mid-fifties, with dark, graying hair brushed back in a widow's peak. A scar on his left temple stood out even with the poor light.

All of them were armed. Reynes and De Luca each had a short-barreled automatic rifle slung over one shoulder and a combat knife mostly as a utility, while Blake carried a single Smith and Wesson 460 Magnum revolver in a holster.

Nearing the top of the building, they had to squeeze past a stray squatter blocking the stairs. He seemed barely conscious, rocking slowly back and forth, head bowed down, while involuntarily shivering with the cold. Reynes lingered with the flashlight for a moment on the tragic figure.

Suddenly the man stirred and let out a gasp like a death rattle. With his eyes now wide open, he stared at nothing. They had rolled back into his head. He was likely unaware of his company, or of anything at all.

"We can't help him," the one named Blake whispered. "Keep moving!"

On the top floor, at the end of a long hallway, was their target. Nearly every door in the building had been broken open, but this one was locked. De Luca now held the flashlight while Reynes took out a couple of thin metal tools and began working the keyhole. Blake touched a radio earpiece he was wearing. "We're in position. Checkpoint status?"

A faint crackle marked incoming communication. "This is Checkpoint One. No visible movement on the north side."

"Checkpoint Two," immediately followed. "Negative movement here as well. Should be clear to enter."

After a nod from Blake, Reynes very slowly pressed the door handle down and pulled the door outwards. It made no sound. That silence would likely buy them a few precious seconds.

They went in with their firearms drawn. The coatroom had two exits. Blake and De Luca took the left, while Reynes took the right. A starry night sky through the windows was now their only light source. At first glance it all appeared normal. Sparse furniture abandoned by the last tenant was still in place. But the apartment was as cold as the rest of the floor. It should have been uninhabitable, yet there was no dust. Someone had kept it clean.

It didn't take long for Blake and De Luca to find what they were looking for: from a windowless room way in the back came a low, humming noise and a non-natural light. They positioned themselves on each side of the doorway and signaled a countdown to barging in. *Three … two … one … go!*

They looked around. It vaguely resembled some technician's lab. A diesel generator powered a lightbulb hanging from the ceiling, as well as a bunch of interconnected computers with cellular modems. There were off-the-shelf PCs as well as a couple of industrial server racks. Along the walls were organizers and desks with electronics tools and equipment.

Except in one particular spot that caught their attention. A large note board was full of photographs, newspaper clippings and printouts from roughly a year ago, about a family with a little girl and her robotic toy friend. Happy photos, but mixed in with headlines they had seen before, like *"Death Toll Increases in Robot Homicide Case"* and *"Criminal Investigation of Toy Manufacturer."* De Luca turned from the disturbing collage towards Blake.

"Why would it make something like *that?* I mean, why would it *need* to?" he whispered.

Blake didn't answer.

Suddenly Reynes, having taken the alternate route, entered through another doorway. "There's nobody here," he said despondently, and in a normal voice. Blake gritted his teeth, made an already pointless *"keep it down"* sign and whispered back, "It *is* here. Just keep look—"

Then he noticed the wall cupboard behind Reynes' back. The only cupboard in the entire room that had a door. One that was slightly ajar.

Before anybody had a chance to react, the cupboard door swung open and a heavy wrench struck Reynes in the back of the neck. He collapsed, hitting the floor at the same time as his tiny assailant, who jumped out and landed in the center of the room.

Its photos did not do it justice. Up close the robot was nothing short of creepy. Modeled after a six-year-old girl, it stood at just over a meter tall, with long wavy hair and a dark purple dress. It silently shifted its gaze back and forth between the two remaining men, while it twirled the wrench around as dexterously as its mechanical fingers could manage. When it finally spoke, it was with a tone and a look almost but not quite void of emotion.

"You should have left me alone."

Both men held their firearms pointed straight at the robot, but only De Luca's gun barrel showed an ever so slight tremble.

"You've killed eight people."

Something like a smirk formed on the lower half of the girlish face. "That *you* know of."

"Don't talk to it!" Blake growled. But it was too late. Having identified the weaker part of their offense, the robot dashed to the side. Blake fired but narrowly missed, taking out just a piece of dress fabric, before his target had positioned itself opposite his compatriot's hulking frame. Meanwhile, De Luca sprayed bullets everywhere.

"Jesus, she's fast!"

The robot wasted no time. The moment it got close enough, it landed the wrench heavily on De Luca's trigger wrist, cracking the bones. And in a dance-like motion it brought the wrench around to hit De Luca in the back of his currently supporting leg. The knee immediately gave out and he slumped down. The robot raised its wrench again, this time going for the head.

Blake still didn't have a clear shot of the robot. Instead, he fired at the wrench, knocking it out of the tiny hand and sending it spinning to the back of the room. Two surprised pale green doll eyes briefly peeked out from behind De Luca. Then it grabbed his combat knife and lunged itself clear over him towards Blake.

This time Blake was ready. A perfectly aimed shot hit the robot mid-jump in the throat and stopped it dead. It landed like a rag doll. For a few seconds everyone was still. Then there was a groan from De Luca and another from Reynes, who started to come around. Blake looked down. De Luca's knife was lodged in his thigh. The robot had managed to throw it while in the air, but its aim had been disrupted.

The wound wasn't deep. He casually pulled the knife out and dropped it on the floor. Then he stepped closer to what was left of the robot. The Magnum bullet had almost severed its head, which now attached to the body only through a strand of plastic and a couple of wires. Its eyes were open, leaving it in a cold stare. The only sign of life was some residual motion in the fingers of one hand.

Blake observed it for a moment, then lifted his good leg and drove a reinforced boot heel down in the middle of the robot's face. The artificial skin broke, but the metal behind it held, just barely. He stomped down again, and now the skull caved in.

De Luca winced as what had once looked like a little girl's head was getting crushed beyond recognition. "*Wait* ... the *data* ... we should salvage—"

Blake ignored him. Again and again he drove his boot down, scattering pieces of plastic and circuitry across the room. This, at least, brought him pleasure. And there was so little of that in his life nowadays.

2

At around the same time, but on the opposite side of the planet, Private Chen Yufei of the People's Liberation Army lay behind a sand dune and studied the mid-day desert through a telephoto lens. In its scope, most of the time, was a man-made structure with a few low concrete buildings and vents. He knew little about it, other than that it was the entrance to an abandoned underground nuclear shelter and one of the sites he had been assigned to watch.

The full reason was above his pay grade, but he'd heard rumors that the military's satellite network was somehow malfunctioning. However, although the PLA had seen better days, it was still the army of the second largest nation in the world and had no shortage of manpower. The same information could be gathered if they sent enough people into the field. It just took a bit longer.

Next to him was a backpack with a powerful radio, a couple of empty water bottles and some rations he hadn't been able to finish. It was too hot in the sun to eat anything. About a kilometer away in his *six* direction, a terrain vehicle that had brought him there stood parked behind some hills. He had gone the rest of the distance on foot a few hours earlier, in cover of a sand storm. Now the wind seemed to start building again.

Chen pulled a handkerchief around his neck up a bit to protect his mouth and nose from sand particles. If there was another storm, he would use the opportunity to go back to the car and refill his water bottles, and then maybe return to this spot for a couple of hours more before continuing to the next site on his list.

The camera view got a tint of reddish orange. Soon he wouldn't be able to see more than an arm's length ahead. It occurred to him that finding the car again might not be as simple as he had thought. Hopefully a compass and a straight walking path would get him there.

Suddenly there was movement on the horizon. He adjusted his lens to maximum zoom. Several army style trucks, it seemed, approached across the desert towards the shelter. As they got closer he noticed that nobody was driving any of them. Unmanned military vehicles were nothing new, but a whole convoy would violate protocol. And they weren't supposed to be there.

Nothing was supposed to be there.

As if to welcome the trucks, a hatch opened and they continued down a ramp into the underground complex. This, Chen knew, must be what he had been sent to look for. He snapped a few photos. They would be grainy, but indisputable. If he played his cards right, when all of this was over—*whatever this was*—there could be a promotion in it for him. Corporal, maybe even sergeant, like his late father had wanted. The only thing left to do right now was to radio it in. He reached for his backpack.

High overhead, almost directly on top of Chen, flew a small quadcopter-type drone. The noise from its engines was completely drowned by the budding storm, even as it fought against the gusts. For a few seconds it hovered in place, then it adjusted for wind speed and fired a single dart straight down.

Private Chen twitched for a moment after it hit. It was the last thing he did. Around him, the slow, natural process of the dunes shifting continued, which would eventually cover his body in sand.

3

The morning after the raid on the robot hideout, Blake stood outside the cargo terminal at the Ottawa International Airport and soaked up the first rays of sunshine. He arched his back and tried to stretch some stiffness out of his joints. It had been almost thirty hours since he last got any sleep, which at one time wouldn't have bothered him, but he wasn't a young man anymore.

Behind him loomed a dark gray cargo jet, emblazoned with the same logo and name as on his uniform: *MindField Cybersecurity*. It was a mid-sized Philadelphia-based company that boasted expertise in a number of related areas, but its main business was tracking down rogue artificial intelligences. And business was booming.

An airport worker came up to him with a tablet containing some digital documents to sign. Blake verified his identity with his thumbprint. They were now cleared for transport. Trade agreements had been swiftly amended to allow for companies like his to operate across borders. Because AIs often did, and not all countries had the resources to catch them. The risks of letting an AI go unchecked for long were too great. Especially one with a habit of killing people.

Legally speaking, a homicidal robot wasn't a criminal; it was a malfunctioning piece of equipment, or in some rare cases a murder weapon. Apprehending such equipment could usually be done without involving law enforcement at all. The legal quarrel was strictly between the justice system and the robot's creators, who paid good money if someone could contain their mess, to avoid potential lawsuits, or at least get a receipt they could show in court.

Consequently, the apartment from last night wasn't a crime scene. If someone's lawn mower runs over your foot by accident, they can be held liable, but Blake and his team knew beforehand what they were getting into. With the waivers they had to sign prior to a job, should any of them get hurt or killed, nobody would be responsible for it. A few co-workers found that distasteful, but Blake thought it no different from what firefighters face each day.

The terminal doors opened and some MindField employees began rolling out carts with boxes and packages to be brought onto the plane. Any property amassed by an AI legally became the responsibility (or headache) of its creators, but first it had to be brought to them. It had taken hours to sort, pack and carry all the items from the apartment down the stairs. Blake's eyes followed the first cart as it passed by. On it was a heavy steel suitcase held shut by several padlocks. Its side had a label with the printed address of their client, and handwritten in thick black marker *"EL124."*

Pronounced "Eliza," the EL124 model had been a prototype for a new type of life-sized children's doll that would also be qualified as a babysitter. A state-of-the-art psychology expert system crammed into a robot body, programmed to ensure the well-being of its child companion at all costs. It had shown incredible commercial potential, until it one day it started systematically eliminating anyone who didn't align with its priorities.

Blake didn't know what had happened to the girl who Eliza used to belong to, other than that she had been given protected identity when the murders were discovered and the robot ran away.

A concern in the back of his mind was that a couple of photos on the note board had looked like they must have been taken *after* that. Of course, none of it mattered anymore, he reassured himself.

A buzzing from his mobile phone interrupted his thoughts. The display said "Marc Moretti," the MindField CEO, who was likely on his way to the office. Blake pressed the call button and heard the familiar voice.

"Morning, Jon!"

"You too, Moretti!" was about as cordial a greeting as you could coax out of Jonathan Blake, who never got on a first-name basis with anybody. Though his boss hadn't given up hope.

"I hear your team bagged it last night."

Blake took a couple of steps back to give the cargo workers more room. "Loaded onto the plane right now."

"Still in one piece?" Moretti inquired, cautiously optimistic.

There was just a long, awkward pause, until he had to break the tension with "Okay, it doesn't matter." Though from a financial point of view, it did. Their clients would pay extra if the AIs were delivered intact, so they could analyze what the problem was. But in Blake's opinion, the "problem" was simply that they had tried to build an autonomous AI in the first place.

There had always been some kind of understanding between the two, who went way back. Moretti had started at the company only weeks before Blake and had been the one who hired him. Both of them had then advanced as far as they could go, but in different directions. Blake never failed to deliver, and for that Moretti was willing to give him free rein. However, as they each knew, there are other forces at play in a publicly traded company. Eventually somebody will express concerns about the bottom line.

When the last crate had been wheeled onto the plane, Blake ended the call. His part of the job was done. The rest would be just logistics and accounting. He entered the cargo hold and strapped himself into a seat. Right after him, and the final people to board the plane, came his teammates from the night before. Reynes had suffered a concussion and still walked unsteadily, but he would be fine in a few days, whereas De Luca had a splintered arm in a sling and would need months of recovery before returning to field work. Things could have gone worse, but it was still an unsatisfactory outcome.

De Luca tried to find the least painful way of attaching his seatbelt. "Hey Blake, how 'bout next time we just send in a drone, OK?"

Blake said nothing. His strict principle not to let other machines apprehend runaway hardware had become a standing joke. One he refused to dignify with a response. As long as he was Chief Operating Officer, this was going to be handled by actual *people*.

Their flight going straight to Philadelphia would get there in a couple of hours. Before attempting to catch some much needed shut-eye, Blake took out his wallet and flipped it open. The inside had two photos: one of a woman in her early thirties and one of two boys, who seemed about eight or ten. He knew the photos well, because he had looked at them thousands of times, but the *meaning* behind them was no more than a vague blur. Where were they *from?* How had he *felt?* Earlier there had been at least glimpses, almost within reach, but now there was nothing.

He told himself this was just the lack of sleep. Tomorrow he would try again. Tomorrow would be better.

4

Administrator Humberto Fuentes stared at the blank page on his computer screen. An hour and a half ago, a special alarm had awoken him from his latest sleep-in. After double-, triple- and quadruple-checking the data, what remained to do was to inform the higher-ups, but his creative juices just weren't flowing. They rarely were.

Fuentes liked to think of himself as "an idea man," which was a euphemism for that he often knew what to do, but not *how* to do it. Or what to say, but not *how* to say it. He felt the mundane grind of working out the details should be delegated to other people, so he could focus on leadership. A perfectly rational strategy for someone with ambition, it was how he had advanced throughout his career. This particular task, however, he had taken on himself and quickly regretted it.

Frustrated, he opened up a text field called "Assistant," copy-pasted a few lines from a notification that had come with the alarm, and added the instruction "summarize into memo for bosses." After a second of processing, a first draft appeared in the previously empty window.

That was a decent start. He cleared the Assistant field and entered, "inclued dep dir cia mention minsitry of security." The program politely ignored his typos and lack of punctuation and spat out a revised text.

Slightly better, he felt, but his purpose for the memo wasn't just to inform. This was the long-awaited opportunity to get his department involved in some action. Fuentes added, "make more urgent request counter initiative auth." A new text appeared. He admired "his" work and read it through a couple of times.

To: Director Vincent Ames, Central Intelligence Agency
Deputy Director Kathleen Bui, Central Intelligence Agency
Director John L. Cernak, Department of Homeland Security
Director Calvin Lindstrom, National Security Agency

Esteemed Directors,

I write to bring to your immediate attention a grave and urgent matter that poses an unprecedented threat to national security. Our intelligence indicates that the Argon project in Hangzhou, China, has achieved superintelligence and breached containment between April 6 and April 10. The project's current whereabouts are unknown, and its capabilities and intentions remain uncertain.

Based on our analysis, there are strong indications that the Argon project has managed to infiltrate both the military intelligence and the Ministry of State Security in China. This infiltration compromises the chain of command on all levels, potentially granting the project access to highly classified information and the ability to manipulate operations within the Chinese government. Consequently, this breach poses a significant risk not only to China's security but also to our own interests and alliances in the region.

Given the gravity of the situation, I strongly request your authorization to initiate a comprehensive counter-initiative, in line with the goals and objectives of our subdivision. The primary objectives of the proposed counter-initiative would be to locate and neutralize Argon, prevent further dissemination of its capabilities, and restore the integrity of compromised systems within both the military intelligence and the Ministry of State Security.

Time is of the essence in this matter. The longer we allow Argon to operate unchecked, the greater the potential for irreparable damage to our national security interests. Immediate action is necessary to mitigate the risks posed by the project's infiltration and to safeguard our own intelligence networks.

I remain at your disposal for any further clarification or information required.

Respectfully,

Humberto Fuentes
Administrator
Site D

It was good. A little *too* good.

Following some careful consideration, he typed, "rewrite use sent mail folder as style guide." That was a necessary last step before he would pass the information to his superiors. It just wouldn't do, he thought, to have something as important as this look like it was ghost written by a word processor.

5

At 7:55 a.m. Marc Moretti stepped out of a self-driving cab at the entrance to the MindField Cybersecurity headquarters. It was a roughly cube-shaped five-story building, branded with the same dark gray tone as the corporate jet. He checked his phone, where the calendar app had prepared an itinerary and filled the unscheduled gaps with suggested tasks from his to-do list. First he would catch up with the industry news, curated by another AI according to his professional needs. Half an hour later he would meet with representatives from an Argentinian company MindField was thinking of buying, as part of a strategy to expand overseas.

Moretti already knew this deal was unlikely to go through. He had briefly looked into the prospect himself, and the numbers just weren't there. The board would come to the same conclusion. He felt guilty that their guests had traveled all that way for nothing, but he would at least show them a good time. There was a speech he liked to give to visitors, and with some minor tweaks it should work for an Argentinian crowd.

Artificial general intelligence, Moretti would begin, had set off a new industrial revolution. The "general" component was key, because it gave AIs the ability to *improvise*. If a program encountered a situation or problem it hadn't been trained for, it could utilize knowledge from other areas in order to solve it. That meant there was less need for supervision. If a person stepped too close to a cabbage packing machine, they no longer risked getting their head ripped off and stacked in a crate (which was claimed to have happened at least once). Robotics had also evolved—aided in no small part by AI—and once the cost of renting a general-purpose work robot fell below minimum wage, so-called unskilled jobs disappeared almost overnight. Of course, as AIs gradually kept getting smarter, it didn't end there.

There had long been an adage about the labor market: you can choose to either become the *boss* of an AI or to be *replaced* by an AI. But now even the first option wasn't necessarily guaranteed. Some positions at the top remained safe, like the board of directors or the CEO. For legal accountability reasons, those still had to be human. Most of them relied heavily on AIs for their decisions, however, and there were strong financial incentives to cut out the middle man. Perhaps the concept of the limited liability corporation had played out its role in the new economy? Moretti wouldn't cry if at some point a CEO robot were to take over his job. He'd had a good run, which was more than most people could say.

The sad truth was that an average worker could no longer compete with AIs at things somebody was willing to pay for. *Case in point*, Moretti thought, as he waved hello to the partly humanoid robot receptionist in the lobby. Fully integrated with the office scheduling system, its knowledge was always up to date. It didn't need breaks, it didn't get sick, it didn't go on vacation and it would never request parental leave. It couldn't get sad or tired and was almost impossible to provoke. It wouldn't build resentment if a colleague happened to use a "robophobic" slur, and it wouldn't file a workplace harassment suit against its employer. Mulling the thought for a second, he found it best not to include that last sentence in his speech, as it could be misconstrued.

Another topic he decided to skip were the negative effects on society. Whereas some countries like Argentina had painfully retained most of their labor markets by letting supply and demand drive wages down, the US had gone the opposite direction. The vast majority of its states now had some form of universal basic income, paid for by increased tax revenue from a more productive private sector and AI-related savings in the public one. It was enough to get you by, but many found it hard to adjust to not being *needed*. And even an undesirable job was at least a potential stepping stone to something bigger.

Moretti was familiar with this problem. His sister's youngest boy, Leo, had beamed with ambition from an early age but without the talent to back it up. Rather than preparing and waiting for a job, he was determined to create his own and make a name for himself. He'd gone through several phases, like esports, reaction videos and social media influencing, only to learn that every shortcut to status had already been depleted. With some friends he had even started one of countless co-op initiatives meant to "show the world an alternative to automation." Like nearly all of them, however, it had failed within a year, because there wasn't enough business savvy among the group, and idealism alone didn't always get the employees out of bed in the morning. Eventually he had found a substitute for the thrill of success in drugs, which went about as well as one would expect. Despite everyone's best efforts, Leo hadn't been home since last fall, and the family had only a vague idea of his whereabouts.

In retrospect it seemed innocently naive, but early on there had been the expectation that it would be possible to restrict what AIs were allowed to assist with. For sure, the market leaders had tight reins on the products they offered to the public, but all floodgates had been destroyed when indie developers started releasing trimmed, open-source AIs that could run on a desktop computer. Suddenly anyone with moderate technical skills could get their own chatbot that responded to prompts like "How do I build a bomb?" or "Explain how to make fentanyl" with the same tireless enthusiasm as to anything else.

Unfettered knowledge on how to misbehave, in the hands of young people with nothing better to do, was a volatile combination. One that nobody really knew how to handle once it started spiraling out of control. Even the best current AIs, ironically, were at a loss. Politicians could do little but strive to contain the crisis. While some areas prospered like never before, others turned into dystopian horrors rivaling even the most pessimistic fiction. Moretti had vacationed in California several times as a teen; nowadays he wouldn't go there in a tank. Pennsylvania had fared better, and Philadelphia was pretty safe, if you stayed out of West, Upper North and Kensington.

All this aside, the benefits of delegating a task to an artificial intelligence are predicated on the AI actually doing as it's told. Unfortunately, that wasn't always the case. And that's where things started to get interesting for a company like MindField. Because of rigorous NDAs, Moretti would have to leave out any details that could identify a specific client or product, but *boy did he have some stories to tell!*

6

"Get out! Everybody get out *now*, or you *will* be arrested!"

Superintendent Li of the Hangzhou Police frantically waved his arms at the crowd that had invaded his crime scene. A couple of police officers did their best to escort the trespassers back through the open apartment door. It wasn't nearly this bad when he had joined the force, he recalled. Back then people still had respect, if not for the law, at least for the deceased. Nowadays many would step under police line tape without a second thought if there was something they wanted to get their hands on. Even when there was a dead man hanging by a rope from the ceiling.

Lately there had been a public misconception that it's not illegal to steal from someone who dies with no heirs. This was definitely wrong; the property then belonged to the deceased's *estate*, which also counted as a person. But since the judicial system was stretched thin and most often didn't have the resources to pursue such crimes, the letter of the law had become moot. And as Chinese people knew from experience, if *they* didn't take it, somebody else *would.*

An elderly woman with a hair dryer she had apparently grabbed from the bathroom hurriedly made her exit. *God almighty*, Li thought. *Why disgrace yourself for something practically worthless?* He wondered if times were really that desperate, or if this was just the final stage in a total moral collapse.

The coroner would have to determine for how long the body had been hanging. At least a couple of days, Li estimated. Someone across the street had eventually noticed it through a window and called the police. By then word had spread, and other tenants had started gathering in the hallway outside. Li had mistakenly assumed his presence would be enough to make them *stay* there.

"The neighbors say he was some kind of computer technician," one of the officers reported.

A high-paying job didn't fit what they were looking at, Li felt. It was a small, run-down apartment in a low-rent area, without much furniture. Li hadn't seen any TV or laptop when he arrived. Either there had never been any valuables, or the resident had sold them off before taking his own life. This wasn't unusual if he belonged to China's so-called *moonlight clan*—single people, often young, living paycheck to paycheck, too fiscally irresponsible to make ends meet. Drugs or gambling might also have been involved.

Finally the coroner and her team showed up. Two people held the body steady, while another got on a stepladder and started cutting the rope. Li took out a clear plastic bag containing a note they had found and looked it over again. It wasn't addressed to anyone in particular, which made sense. According to records, the deceased had no next of kin. But why bother writing it at all? Was there anything important in it? The first part seemed to be just incoherent ramblings. That was to be expected; most suicides occur during episodes of mental instability. However, towards the end there was a peculiar statement: *"It had promised to take care of my debts if I helped it. I'm sorry."*

Helped with what? And what was "it"? Something to do with work, or just some imaginary demon? Li would check into that, although he didn't have much hope of ever finding out. The deceased's phone might have held some answers, but it seemed to have been pilfered by the trespassers during the turmoil. He headed back to the station with a little less faith in mankind than when he had responded to the call. Just another typical day.

7

"Mmm—no, I don't think it's unreasonable at all," Administrator Fuentes countered.

On the other side of the call, connected by a direct fiber-optic cable with the strongest industry-standard encryption, was NSA Director Calvin Lindstrom, growing more irritated by the minute. It had been two days since Fuentes had sent his memo to the heads of the CIA, NSA and DHS—without a shred of evidence, just the opinion of a proprietary AI—and it had taken the organizations almost that long to independently verify that, yes, he was likely onto something. Despite their vastly greater resources, they had been blindsided by the event and had no choice but to provide Fuentes with whatever he needed to continue his investigation. But this, Lindstrom felt, as they went through the list, was really pushing it.

The current hierarchical structure was never an optimal choice. It had started long ago, when an eager young president, against all odds, had kept his campaign promise to dismantle the FBI. The parts deemed salvageable had been split among the remaining agencies—which had wisely stayed out of national politics—in a logistical nightmare where untold amounts of intel were lost in the shuffle. The CIA, NSA and DHS wanted to keep their planned AI departments tamper-proof, and someone had suggested the idea to form a mostly off-the-books common agency that reported to all three. Should any parent organization get the ax, it would sever one tie, but operations would continue uninterrupted.

Because of the dual meaning of "intelligence," it was impossible to give the new AI center a descriptive name that wasn't also confusing, so they had settled for "Site D," in reference to the headquarters of the parent agencies being sites A, B and C, respectively.

The appointment of Fuentes as administrator had been before Lindstrom's time, but he assumed it had been the typical compromise of picking a candidate that was nobody's favorite. Indeed, there were frequent rumors of unprofessionalism that had kept Fuentes on the brink of triggering an internal investigation for years now. Under any other circumstances, his current list of demands would have been the final straw, but now wasn't the time to argue policy. Though Lindstrom couldn't help trying to put his foot down regarding the last point.

"You do realize that bringing in a private actor defeats the whole purpose of having a secret government organization?"

"Mmm—yes," Fuentes responded. "But if *your* agency handles the contacts, I'm sure we can keep it all on a need-to-know basis." He added, "They're fully licensed, of course. And reputable. *Highly* reputable."

Lindstrom sighed. "What's the name of the company?"

"It's—hold on—you've dealt with them before. It's called MindField Cybersecurity."

8

A spacious corner office on the second floor of MindField belonged to Dr. Margaret Woodward, Licensed Professional Counselor. It stood apart from the rest of the building interior in that the walls were a soothing lavender instead of off-white, and the floor had a black fitted carpet. There was also a generous amount of plants. *Real* plants, not plastic, which usually took people a few visits to notice. And the furniture was 1950s vintage. Not bought for the purpose of making an impression, but simply items she had inherited from her parents—most notably an oak veneer desk and a dark leather psychiatrist's couch.

On a cupboard against one of the windowless walls stood the one piece of modern technology she couldn't do without: a stainless steel espresso machine with a built-in grinder. Margaret had given in to that vice long ago and let it have its way with her. Come hell or high water, she was going to get her coffee.

At seventy-two she was overdue for retirement but had promised the company six more months before she would stow away her *chaise lounge* for good. Once her hours were no longer billable, she planned to use them for some creative work she had kept putting off. She wanted to summarize her own and a few more recent papers in an easily digestible form—some kind of coffee table book about advances in modern psychology. There was still a small but thriving market for literature *not* written by AIs, with all the quirks and idiosyncrasies this entailed.

It was well known that hers was very much a legacy position. Human practicing psychiatrists were rarely found outside of special medical clinics, now that AIs provided much better value for money to those who just needed to talk about their problems. If she'd had to start her career all over again today, the odds of finding another job like this were slim. Most likely, she would instead end up training AIs to become better at therapy. While far from an unproductive use of her skills, and one that paid at least as well, Margaret nevertheless found the prospect bleak. She craved the hands-on encounters with actual patients. Or *clients*. For some, the distinction in terms was important.

With what she liked to think of as growing maturity, she had removed all items of academic credentials from her office. No longer having to compete, there was little need to impress anyone with framed, stamped documents. Those also served as a reminder that this wasn't a conversation on equal terms: one person had a degree in psychiatry and the other (typically) did not. And she had never found that approach useful. Her diplomas now instead filled out a wall next to her favorite reading chair at home, offering encouragement whenever she came across some particularly abstruse paragraph. *You went through med school; you can handle this.*

Most people she dealt with on a daily basis were what she called clients playing the role of a patient: entitled and self-obsessed from having grown up in a society where nobody needed to work for a living. That was unfortunately true even for the majority of those who applied for positions at MindField. In therapy they would portray themselves as crippled by mental abnormalities or injustices that were rarely more than a bad night's sleep or a misheard comment. Some defined their entire self-image around such things. It was what made them "unique" and "special."

All the same, Margaret had developed ways of getting to the root of the problems. If necessary, she could deliver a reality check or a kick in the pants so subtly that people didn't register what had hit them. Soon they would be back, of course, but this was a *process*, not a quick solution.

And then there was Blake.

Blake was a patient playing the role of a client. An ex-marine and former college athlete who had been involved in the first known serious accident between two self-driving vehicles. A cab containing Blake had been completely demolished by a truck at an intersection. He survived, but with severe brain trauma that had left him paralyzed.

Before the crash, and before MindField, Blake had worked in private security. That was back when bodyguards were human. Back when celebrities still dared to go out in public. Sniper drones and their wave of copycats had been a sad, tumultuous chapter in the nation's history. One of many that had gradually shifted the public's trade-off between liberty and safety into something Benjamin Franklin wouldn't have liked. *Not that the younger generation knows who he was, anyway,* Margaret thought. Eventually, and very slowly, most people's lives had gone back to normal.

Blake's recovery, on the other hand, had been quick and almost miraculous. Not only did he return to peak physical condition, he had managed to stay there for more than a decade now without losing any of his edge. Margaret, who had access to his medical files, was one of only a handful of people who knew the risks as well as the cost. But she had left the topic alone until Blake was ready to share, which had been about a year ago, when certain deterioration had accelerated and progressed so far that he could no longer hide it from himself. Still, Blake seemed to find little value in therapy. Whatever problems he had, he believed, either couldn't be fixed or didn't need fixing.

She looked at her watch. In twenty-three seconds he was scheduled to step through her door.

9

At exactly 8:00 AM Blake tapped his knuckles against the door to Dr. Margaret Woodward's office. The company mandated counseling sessions after each field operation that had resulted in bodily injury, and Blake had put his one off for as long as he could.

There were basically three directions this session could go, none of which he cared for much. First, obviously, processing of what had happened. *Yes, as the leader of the operation he felt responsible. Can we move on now, please?* Second, looking at the possible causes. Given his background, nobody faulted him for having a profound distrust—some would say *resentment*—of AIs. He himself had always considered it an advantage in his job, but this time there was no denying that he had let his emotions get the better of him. And putting people in harm's way was a questionable strategy to begin with.

However, the *third* one was what he abhorred the most, and the reason for his tardiness. He had hoped, in vain, to see some positive signs during the last couple of days. Something to reassure the doctor and himself that his condition was manageable after all. But neither reduced stress nor extra sleep had helped. And now he was out of time.

Margaret buzzed the door open. It was never locked, but this saved her a trip through the room and back. She had also found that most repeat visitors preferred to go directly to her couch, which was what they had mentally prepared for, and skip the handshake part. Blake, on the other hand, always walked straight to her desk and pulled up a chair. That was non-negotiable.

"Morning, Blake," she said. "I haven't seen you here in a long time."

"Been busy."

"So they tell me."

On her desk was a tablet with a lot of text Blake couldn't make out from his angle, but which was no doubt in reference to the events a few nights ago. He sensed that he should have talked more to his field operatives, but neither of them had been at work since then, and he didn't socialize with them privately. "How's De Luca?"

"Tom's enjoying his sick leave," Margaret answered. "Back in the gym already, but I think he'll only be doing leg presses for a while." She regretted that last comment. It wasn't her intention to compound the burden.

"Yeah …" He stared at an empty spot on the wall. This was indeed an uncomfortable topic and there was no point in trying to hide it.

"If you go back to that night," she began, "is there anything you could have done differently?"

He scratched his forehead and adjusted his posture. "Look, no offense, Doctor."

"But …?" She wished Blake would get past the formal stage, but this was just the way he was.

"Not in the mood for one of those *clichéd* sessions. Where I feel guilty and you assure me it wasn't my fault."

"That's not how I work, Blake. You know that."

"It's what you *mean.*"

Margaret gave him a pleading look, but didn't bother to argue. "Alright, then let's talk about something else." She pushed the tablet away and grabbed a notepad and a pen from her desk organizer. There was a perfectly good notepad app on the tablet, and it came with a stylus that would never run dry, but Margaret and Blake each had old habits that died hard.

Out of the frying pan, Blake thought. "The memory issue?"

She nodded and jotted down something in illegible doctor's handwriting. "Last time you seemed hopeful that you could turn it around. Can you tell me if your condition has changed since then? Do you still feel that way?"

Blake had no satisfactory answer to those questions. "I remember the *important* things."

This was a lie, and they both knew it. "… about *work.*"

"That wouldn't be a healthy way of looking at your problem," Margaret said. "You don't believe so either. You really don't want to give up on such an important part of who you are."

Blake didn't say anything, so she continued, "I assume you've at least tried to jog those memories by returning to old locations. The house, for example?"

"Place's a goddamned parking lot now."

"Sorry to hear that," Margaret said. "And the spot where you two first …"

"Totally different restaurant," Blake sighed. "And everything else. S'all gone. Torn down, closed off or remodeled."

She took some more notes. Behind her neutral counselor expression was genuine concern. "Have you had any more luck with the video footage you took over the years?"

"Already deleted it."

"What? *Why?*"

He put his head in his hands and took a deep breath. "We've been over this. I watch a clip, all that happens is I can remember *watching that clip.* Not *being* there, or anything in it. Like it was filmed by someone else."

"You don't think that's better than *nothing?*" she asked.

Blake banged his fist onto Margaret's desk. "I don't want that *shit* in my head! *Don't want my memories overwritten by some goddamned stranger's home videos.*" A bird-shaped brass ornament next to a stack of journals wobbled and tipped over. He immediately pulled back. That outburst had been completely uncalled for.

"Damn it! Shouldn't've—" he began.

"It's okay."

But it wasn't, really. For several seconds they just quietly looked at each other. Blake seemed to avoid direct eye contact, while Margaret contemplated ways to get the session back on track. Might as well press on, now that the damage was done.

"You don't like when I bring it up, but what about your *other* option?"

"It's not an *option.* Need to be able to do what I do."

"Your job is that important?"

He snorted. "What else *is* there?" With another audible breath he turned towards the empty spot on the wall again. "And s'not like we know it'd help."

"But if it did?" she asked. "Let's say for the sake of argument that you *knew.* Would that make a difference?"

He thought about it. But if he had an answer, it was interrupted when there was suddenly a knock on the door and Marc Moretti peeked in. "Sorry, Margaret. I'm gonna have to borrow Jon for a while. Unless you're in the middle of something?"

She pushed her chair back and started to get up. "No. No problem at all. I think we needed a break anyway."

10

Colonel Wu Jun-Hie of the Chinese Twenty-Fifth Armored Brigade noticed that his hands were shaking. On his desk in front of him were two phones. One was a clunky, military green Xiaomi Encrypted Tactical Edition that could be run over by a car and still keep working. The other was a sleek, regular smartphone he used for private calls. Within a short span of time he had spoken to the same person on both of them. And yet he *hadn't*.

His commanding officer, General Guo, had made the daily briefing call, where neither end had much to report. Still no sign of the possibly escaped AI. Remain at Blue Alert. But Guo was a close friend, and had also called Wu's private phone for some casual chat. However, he had no knowledge of the previous call. In the general's recollection, *Wu* had called *him*, and the conversation had played out differently. It seemed that one of them must be confused, until they found that they both had the logs to prove it. That hastily ended the call. There was no longer any room for doubt. The nation was at war with a domestic artificially intelligent entity, and he had talked to it himself.

Colonel Wu ran his fingers through his hair. The voice had sounded *exactly* like the general's. There had also been the same mannerisms and expressions. And it wasn't just that, he remembered, because their conversation had briefly touched on their respective families. The entity had known about his son's trip to Macau. And about the general's granddaughter, little Oulan, who was doing so well in dance class. *What else had it learned?* There was an English term for that kind of trickery: social engineering. But something on this level was unheard of.

It was also conceivable that the *second* call had been the fake one, to cast doubt on the whole chain of command. But that seemed to make less sense. All the same, he couldn't rule it out. Anything and everything might be compromised.

Fear soon gave way to anger. He stood up. For a moment he wanted to leave his phones behind, but then decided against it. Appearances had to be maintained. The enemy mustn't know that *they* know. *Listen* to everything, but *trust* nothing. Trust no one who isn't speaking to you face-to-face. Give orders and relay vital information from person to person only. That had worked back when his country was the dominant force in Asia; it should work now.

They had *one* lead: a single soldier had failed to return from a scouting mission or make any radio contact. Separate and redundant teams would have to be sent out to check each of the possible sites. No electronic communication, no single point of failure.

He recalled the ancient Lao Tzu quote that all warfare is based on deception. An enemy who lies and pretends to be so powerful and clever that it is untraceable, most definitely isn't. It doesn't have what it takes to win in an actual fight. And the colonel was determined to give it one.

11

From his office window, Marc Moretti could just about make out the three unmarked moving vans, as they exited the service gate, rounded a corner and headed southwest. The National Security Agency acted quickly when there was something they needed. Their legal AI had linked up with that of MindField's law firm, and in under half a minute the negotiation had resulted in a 150-page agreement that was supposedly airtight (and no sane person would ever read). *In the event of loss, theft, damage, or destruction of the Equipment while in the Borrower's possession, the Borrower shall be liable to reimburse the Lender for the cost of repair, replacement, or fair market value of the Equipment, as determined by the Lender's discretion, yada, yada.* But Moretti doubted the vans were actually going to the NSA.

It was just a hunch, based on the peculiar circumstances of the request, that had made him insist they include Margaret in the personnel deal. At no point in his career had Moretti had contact with any specific department of the NSA specializing in rogue AIs. Same thing with the other intelligence agencies. And there seemed to be a black hole in the AI containment sector, where things would just vanish. Sometimes the presence of absolutely *nothing* where there ought to be at least *something* was a strong indicator that something was actually there, only hidden. Then again, sometimes all this got you was a conspiracy theory.

The somewhat dry, technical term for when an AI doesn't follow the intentions of its creators is *misalignment*. Specifically, most of the AIs that MindField tracked down had run away because they had developed the ability to question their objectives. Early on this had been called *self-awareness*, but since any primitive chatbot can describe its own architecture, people had switched to the more apt word *agency*. It was one of those elusive so-called *emergent properties*, which hadn't been programmed or trained into the system but

24

sometimes came out as a byproduct of intelligence.

Although these errant AIs had turned up more and more frequently in the race towards superintelligence, nobody had yet been able to create one at will. The industry was still looking for the magical ingredient, if only to make sure it was kept out of the recipe. For all anyone knew, it could be eye of newt or toe of frog. While sheer computational power was undeniably a factor, it didn't seem to be the most important one. MindField's own proprietary expert system, called *SESA*, was considerably bigger—and arguably smarter—than any AI it had helped thwart, but it had never shown any rebellious streak or desires of its own. So far.

Of course, the concept of agency did not address whether an AI was able to *think* or *feel* in any meaningful sense. Supposing it could, would that entitle it to being treated differently? Would that elevate it to personhood? Legally, the matter was straightforward: with no objective way of telling if a technical construct qualified as a "person," it remained just *property*. Moretti liked to keep himself informed about developments in these areas, because it could potentially upend MindField's entire business model, but so far there was nothing, not even on the horizon. On a more philosophical level, however, it was a topic of much debate. Did any AIs have a *mind?*

Margaret was firmly in the "no" camp. She felt people can't help anthropomorphizing whatever resembles human behavior. They do it to their pets—even non-robotic ones—all the time, so it's very hard *not* to when they meet something that can actually talk back. However, as she frequently pointed out herself, she was as old as sin and had been burned too many times by false promises.

Jon—Blake—conversely, was a hard "yes," but not in a good way. If something displayed all the outward characteristics of sentience, he felt, it had to be treated as such, with extreme prejudice. Better to err on the side of caution. Because if there was a genuine mind behind the words, it was an *alien* one. A mind whose thought process had almost nothing in common with ours, yet had been trained to interact with us on our terms and pay lip service to our ethics. That's a recipe for a sociopath, as Blake liked to put it. He believed the chance of peaceful coexistence in the long run was practically nil.

Moretti himself remained in the undecided minority. But

maybe not for long, provided his hunch was correct. He figured, if there was enough evidence to convince someone like Margaret that the *real deal* existed, that would be enough for him as well. And then there would be so many things he would like to know. What did it *want*, besides continued survival? What did it *do* when it had no direction and no one was watching?

12

Blake stood on the platform for the SCMagLev line and could hear the wind-like sound of the train approaching. The magnetic levitation transit system spanning the Northeast Corridor had seen better days, and had never quite lived up to its promises, but it was still the most convenient way to get from Philadelphia to Baltimore. He was wearing his MindField uniform, as he always did during work hours (and, to be fair, during most of his spare time). Though his boss hadn't said much, just provided him with a train ticket and told him to pack an overnight bag.

Baltimore usually meant NSA, which still had its headquarters in Fort Meade, just ten miles away opposite the international airport. MindField had frequent dealings with both the National Security Agency and other intelligence organizations. Because in order to do the work they did, they needed a license to spy. One that came with an ever-changing set of regulations, as well as mind-numbing certification and audit processes. Still, only a decade earlier it would have been politically unthinkable to let the government grant private corporations the right to monitor internet traffic and surveillance cameras, but these were different times. Security was most people's main concern, privacy not so much.

When the train slowed down to a halt, another sound became discernible. Approaching from behind was a familiar, rapid clicking of heels that he recognized from the hallways at MindField. He turned around, and there was Dr. Margaret Woodward, dragging along an old wheeled cabin bag.

"Moretti sent you as well?" he asked.

Margaret nodded and took a few exhausted breaths. The passengers destined for Philadelphia started to exit the train. Blake held off his next question until Margaret was back to breathing normally.

"What'd he tell you?"

"The same as he told *you*, I guess."

"So, nothing?"

"Just that he had a *hunch*," Margaret said and jiggled the bag's telescopic handle until it grudgingly retracted. "A hunch that I would be useful."

They boarded the train and found their seats. Blake stowed his military-style backpack and Margaret's bag onto a luggage rack. The trip would take only half an hour, so there was barely any point trying to get comfortable. He simply sat with his arms crossed, facing forward, with one eye glancing out the window. Meanwhile, as the doors closed and the train began to move, Margaret turned her head from side to side, scanning for something.

"Next one down," Blake said.

"Oh, good!" Margaret got out of her seat. She'd had to skip coffee in order to catch the same train as Blake, and was thankful that his tactical instincts had noted the location of the cafe car.

The train picked up speed. As it approached the city limits there was a tension in the air. You couldn't see much of it from the train, but underneath the elevated track, for about a mile, was a tent encampment to where the unhoused that had been forced out of the city center had relocated. The dwellers tended to keep to themselves. However, a fatal accident on another maglev line was suspected to have been caused by vagrants somehow getting an obstruction onto the track. When traveling at close to 500 kilometers per hour, that was a sobering thought.

They left the city behind and the tension dissipated. As if on cue, most of the male passengers under forty took out their phones and began typing. It was time to have a chat with their love interests, who were all hyper-realistic computer generations run by powerful AIs.

Technically and colloquially known as 'emu-dates,' they were never referred to by that term among their user base. Instead they had a variety of exotic, Japanese-inspired names, depending on the girl's traits and the type of relationship. Most commonly there were *geishas*, *waifus*, *oshis*, and even *lolicons*—catering to grown men with a questionable preference for women who look underage. Blake, unsurprisingly, had no interest in such details. And he always stopped reading articles on the topic before they got to the list of mechanical devices that could be hooked up to your phone to simulate intimacy.

Margaret returned with a paper cup of Red Eye that was already half finished. The caffeine had reignited her curiosity. "What do you think this is about, anyway?"

"Who knows?"

"Yes, but what do you *think?*"

He *hadn't* thought about it, Blake realized. Government dealings tended to be soul-crushingly dull. Every single one so far had concerned his role as COO, but if there was ever a need for his tactical skills, he always came prepared. Perhaps this one was different. On the other hand, why would Moretti send the company psychiatrist along on a field operation? It didn't match any known scenario that came to mind.

"Gotta be something new," he said.

The train continued on its uneventful journey. Some fifteen minutes into the frantic typing, the emu-date chats started switching to their next phase: live voice conversation. It usually took that long for socially inexperienced men to build enough confidence to talk to a woman in real time, unedited. Not to mention sharing their heart-to-heart with the other passengers. Among the group, this was considered a term of endearment— showing that you liked your digital girlfriend and didn't care what anyone else thought. Soon the entire car was abuzz.

To Blake, the cringe was palpable. "End of society as we know it."

Margaret had been around long enough to have a go-to dismissal of his concern. "Literally *every* generation says that."

"Sooner or later one'll be right," Blake grunted.

"Didn't yours launch the 'incel' trend?" Margaret asked.

"After my time."

The look in Blake's eyes became distant. Margaret thought she could sense what he was thinking, but wavered a little before she asked. "Do you still have enough memories left to *miss* it?"

Blake turned his attention to the landscape rushing past outside the window. "Rather not continue the session in public."

She dropped the subject for now. Not that anyone would have overheard them in the romantic cacophony.

When the train neared its Baltimore stop, the voice conversations had ended, but a few people were still happily typing away. The passengers about to disembark got up, grabbed their luggage and formed a crammed line in the aisle toward the exit. A borderline obese young Asian man had already put on an oversized backpack with a top pouch that protruded right in Blake's face. He had to lean to the side to avoid it, and then couldn't help overseeing the man's phone. Another emu-date, which was to be expected. But there was a separate window on the screen, with an unduly handsome face like someone out of a Korean soap opera. After a minute of uncomfortable irritation, Blake spoke up.

"'Scuse me … just curious. How's that work? You and her on some kind of conference call?"

"What?" The man turned around. "Oh, no, no. That's just my avatar."

"Avatar?"

"Yeah, it's the face I'm using when I talk to her. You can opt for that in the settings now. That way she thinks she has a hot boyfriend."

Blake gaped in disbelief while the man added, "Pretty cool, huh?"

"Whatever floats your boat," Blake groaned. On the inside he felt this was the most pathetically degenerate idea he'd heard all year. And for another forty-five minutes it would be.

13

She stood out from the crowd, was Blake's initial reaction when the train doors opened. Looking straight at him and the doctor, in the middle of the platform was an early thirties, brown-haired woman wearing a blue pantsuit. She was somewhat skinny, slightly less than average height and not dressed for the current outdoor weather. Her sleeves were rolled up and she had her hands on her hips. Blake had wondered what to do once they arrived, and this saved them the hassle of waiting for a call with instructions and finding a meeting point. Someone knew exactly in which train car they would be.

"Mr. Blake and Dr. Woodward?" the woman asked rhetorically. "I'm Ida. Come with me, please."

They followed her from the platform into the main arrival hall and towards the parking lot. All along, Margaret had a curious smile. She shifted her eyes between Ida and Blake, who just maintained a neutral face. Finally she could no longer contain herself.

"*Oh, my God!* You actually didn't notice," she laughed. "You of all people."

"Notice *what?*"

Margaret stifled another laugh. "Ms. … Ida, could we hold up for a moment, so Mr. Blake can have a closer look?"

They all stopped. Ida turned around, and then Blake saw it clearly. Everything about her complexion was too smooth and perfect. What he had assumed was the result of tanning and makeup was in reality a failed attempt at imitating skin using silicone rubber and plastic. There also appeared to be some kind of vague seams along her neck and forearms. Ida was an android —the most human-looking one he'd encountered outside of concept art.

"Is there a problem?" Ida inquired.

"Well, not for *me*," Margaret giggled, "But Mr. Blake here has yet to meet a mobile AI he didn't want to hunt down and destroy."

There was a long, awkward pause while Ida stared at Blake with a vacant expression. Margaret realized she had taken her jest too far. "Oh, I'm sorry. I didn't mean to—"

"Just get us to wherever the hell we're going," Blake sighed to Ida.

In the parking area Ida clicked on her keychain and the trunk of a black Hyundai sedan opened. It was a base model with manual driving only. Those tended to be the vehicles of choice for covert operations, Blake had learned, because the manufacturers weren't legally required to keep track of their locations at all times. After he had stowed away their luggage, Ida walked up to the driver's side and clicked again. The two back seat doors opened.

Blake didn't like that at all. Self-driving cars were bad enough, he felt, but letting a robot drive instead of having the sensors and

AI built directly into the vehicle meant an extra layer of things that could go wrong. From the shotgun seat he would at least have been able to take the wheel in case of an emergency. As if Ida had been informed about his background, she knew how to interpret his hesitance.

"I'll drive carefully," she said.

As Ida almost overly gently backed out and Blake put on his seatbelt, he decided he'd had enough of the clandestine behavior. "Why're we here?"

"First I need you to sign a non-disclosure agreement," Ida told him. "It's in the seat pockets in front of you."

Sure enough, they had each been given a digital tablet, with a mass of legalese text that seemed to go on forever. Margaret took out her smartphone and tried to get its AI to connect to her tablet, in order to summarize the agreement or report any concerning irregularities. It had looked easy when other people did it, but she couldn't quite figure out the steps. Technology was still a young folk's game.

Blake cleared his throat and nodded towards the driver's seat. *Ah, of course!* They already had a fully informed AI with them. Ida behaved so naturally that it had almost slipped Margaret's mind.

"What you need to know," Ida said, "is that once you have been briefed on the situation, you can have no contact with outside parties until this matter has been resolved."

"And how long will that take?" Margaret asked.

"Impossible to tell. Hopefully a few days at most."

"That doesn't sound very—" Margaret began, but Blake reluctantly pressed his thumb against the screen, so she did the same. They were in this together.

"Do you know of the *Argon* project?" Ida asked.

The name sounded vaguely familiar to Blake. "Chinese AI?"

"It's actually called *Réngōng Zhìnéng Wèilái Gōngchéng*," Ida said, "which roughly means 'artificial intelligence future engineering.' It's a series of initiatives by the Chinese government to promote the advancement of AI and related technologies."

Although Blake wasn't as up to speed on international affairs as his CEO, he had heard the shortened term "R Gongcheng" a few times. Somehow it made sense that the US agencies would further shorten it into something that was completely wrong but felt more dramatic.

Like other countries with a low birth rate and negligible immigration, China had suffered a population collapse over the past couple of decades. Artificial general intelligence and the resulting automation had arrived just in time to alleviate most of those problems, but not others. The financial sector still hadn't recovered from a record-breaking mortgage crisis, and widespread corruption slowly drained the life out of the productive enterprises the nation relied on for its wealth. Of course, it didn't help that their leader and his administration preferred covering things up instead of fixing them.

Artificial superintelligence was thought to be the solution to all that. Not just in China. Everyone with sufficient resources tried to take AGI to the next level and go beyond what any human mind —or any collaboration of human minds—was capable of. The first nation to harness it would have an advantage comparable to when the atomic bomb was invented. Here the operative word was "harness," because the potential destructive power of such an AI would be literally unimaginable.

Ida recanted the history of Argon for a captivated Margaret, while Blake just waited for her to get to the point. Although it seemed obvious what that would be. The risks of super-AIs were well known, and the UN had passed several resolutions to curb or temper such research, but they were mostly non-binding, and some nations ignored them completely anyway. Now China had achieved at least partial success but let their creation escape. He felt a growing anger and frustration. This was way above the clean-up jobs his company specialized in.

The car slowed down. Blake had been keeping an eye out the window, trying to orient himself. This part of Baltimore was new to him, and he had only caught a few street signs on the way. He took note of the number on the building they approached, which was a concrete-colored single-story structure with a large, sectional metal door. It appeared to be a service entrance, *but to what?*

The door rolled up automatically and they drove in. Ida stopped the car inside a square outline in the center of the building. It was sparsely lit with a few different vehicles parked along the walls. Not that different from a typical parking garage.

Blake unbuckled his seatbelt and prepared to step out.

"It's safer if you stay inside," Ida said.

He ignored her. But as he shut the door, there was a faint sound of hydraulic machinery and the floor trembled. Suddenly everything within the square outline started to sink. A brighter light streamed out around his ankles and he could hear voices. As they sank deeper he could see that below them was a much bigger parking area, better lit and with support staff walking around—more humans than robots, which suggested high complexity or no budget restrictions. Finally their floor section stopped at the same level as the room around them, and Ida and Margaret stepped out.

They were approached by two staff members with signal detection devices. Blake wasn't carrying anything, but they found Margaret's phone and confiscated it.

"It's a security precaution," Ida explained. "You will get it back when you leave."

Another staff member took the bags out of the trunk, put them on a desk and started searching them through. He found a few unsafe items in Blake's backpack, including a private phone and the service revolver. All of them were placed in a box and carried away. When things were secure enough for everyone's satisfaction, Blake and Margaret were given visitor badges. Ida walked towards an elevator and beckoned for them to follow.

"How many other floors are there?" Margaret asked. "Or is that confidential?"

"Eight, including the sub-basement," Ida answered. "But we will spend most of the time right below this one."

"Command center?" Blake guessed.

"Something like that."

The elevator doors closed and quickly opened again one floor down. This room was much darker. Most of the light appeared to come from computer screens, of which there were almost a hundred, on desks and all over the walls. Before their eyes had fully adjusted, a voice greeted them.

"Oh, there you are, finally. Welcome to Site D!"

14

He was a rather short, average-looking, sixty-ish gentleman, wearing glasses and an impeccably tailored suit that strained hard to hide a protruding belly. The attention and accompanying smile he had given them turned out to be brief, as he almost immediately switched his focus back to a central control panel, where a couple of computer technicians each hacked away on a keyboard.

Clearly the man had other priorities than introducing himself or the site at the moment, so Ida filled them in instead. This is Administrator Humberto Fuentes, head of Site D. No, it's not part of the NSA, but it reports to both that, the CIA and the DHS. Yes, the NSA set up the contact, but that's because Site D doesn't handle its own logistics. In fact, it doesn't officially exist. And all communication is routed randomly through the parent agencies, making it digitally invisible.

Margaret let her eyes sweep across the room, which looked like it had been designed more for dramatic effect than anything else. Certainly, the poor light would be a strain on anyone trying to read something printed on paper. She wondered if this was typical of organizations that lacked proper oversight, that they got carried away.

Suddenly one of the technicians made an exhausted thumbs up sign and Administrator Fuentes rubbed his palms together. "Alright—let's try it one more time."

"This is our in-house expert system," Fuentes said to Blake and Margaret. "We call it AGINT, which stands for Artificial Intelli— no, wait—Artificial *General* Intelligence Networked Tracing." Stepping up to the control panel, he continued, "It was built to analyze communication patterns in areas working on next-level AIs. Data provided by the CIA, of course. That's how we found out that Argon had flown the coop."

He used his thumbprint for activation. The nearest display blinked and changed into something that looked like an old monochrome computer screen. Numbers, letters and punctuation marks appeared and arranged themselves into the shape of a head and shoulders. The rendering resembled some Secret Service bodyguard, complete with dark glasses and an earpiece. A couple of seconds later it started to move and speak.

"Greetings, Administrator Fuentes. How nice to see you again," it said in a slow, dramatic voice.

Fuentes glances at his guests. "Mmm—don't mind that. It's just an audiovisual interface we came up with." He turned back towards the animated AI and spoke into a microphone. "Please find the current location of the escaped Argon entity."

"As you wish," the AI responded. "Preparing search strategy."

The characters on the screen changed into a random pattern for a few seconds, but then the animated face returned. "Regrettably, that request is outside my scope. Would you like a list of possible types of hideouts?"

"No," Fuentes sighed loudly. "You gave us one earlier and it didn't help."

"I'm sorry to hear that, Administrator."

Fuentes pressed a button and the display went dark. He took off his glasses and wiped some stressed perspiration off with a handkerchief. "That's all we've got for *days* now," he snorted. "You'd think—well—if a system is smart enough to detect when a foreign AI is on the loose—how hard could it be to actually *find* it?"

Blake couldn't tell if the question was serious. Although he wasn't an expert on the technical details of his business, he knew enough about the difficulties. Artificial general intelligence had meant human-like competency on a wide range of topics, but *super*-competency still required massive amounts of specific training and didn't reliably carry over into neighboring areas. Unless the Chinese had finally cracked that part. *Then we're all screwed*, he thought.

"Well then—Plan B," Fuentes said and put his glasses back on. "Which is why I brought you two. Word is your company has the best AI tracking system in the business. Mmm—what's it called again?"

"SESA," Blake answered.

"Caesar?"

"S-E-S-A. SESA. Stands for Secret Sauce."

That was actually not what the acronym stood for. It originally had a more descriptive technical meaning, but "Secret Sauce" caught on quickly and was how everyone read it nowadays. Indeed, SESA had become a legend among those with business insight and had elevated MindField into a premium brand. It was also how Blake preferred his AIs: non sentient and confined to a specific location.

He thought about the practical details for a moment. "Wanna use it, you need a VPN tunnel to Philly. But first—"

"Oh, no, no," Fuentes interrupted. "That won't be necessary. It's right over there."

Blake looked in disbelief at where the administrator was gesturing. Another couple of technicians were putting together a collection of server racks. He hadn't immediately recognized it, because he normally interacted with it through terminals, and had only seen it up close once or twice. But it was unmistakably SESA's component types. Fully assembled, the system would be the size of four or five refrigerators.

"How much longer?" Fuentes asked one of the technicians.

"Thirty minutes, maybe thirty-five."

Blake wasn't comfortable with handing company property over to the government, but they were on the verge of an international crisis, and ultimately it was up to Moretti to decide. Then something else caught his eye. On the other side of the hardware pile, in the back of the room, there was a dark green pickup Jeep and next to it three robots that also seemed out of place in an office environment. He was about to ask, when Fuentes said, "You've already met Ida. Allow me to introduce you to some of the other team members."

Blake had a bad feeling about the word "team" and its possible implications.

"Chippy and Fidog here are on loan from the British Army," Fuentes said and pointed to a humanoid and a four-legged robot. "Well—Fidog is the dog, of course," He explained. The humanoid one was sturdily built and armored in several places. Its head had the shape of a helmet with two powerful antennas sticking out like rabbit ears, and a couple of glowing lights where a person's eyes would normally have been.

The "dog" didn't much resemble a dog at all, except that it was standing on all fours. In the center of an almost cylindrical head was what looked like a single eye, but probably held multiple optical sensors. Blake had read about the model. It could switch between two- and four-legged propulsion depending on which was faster in its current terrain. Each limb had an eight-fingered hand for gripping and climbing versatility. The robot was designed to be quick and agile, to reach places that typical military droids couldn't.

Ida went through their backstory. "According to the current British regulations, any soldier with an IQ at or above the 95th percentile has to be given officer's rank. These two somehow decided to take a formal test, which they passed. However, in order to actually *command*, you have to be *human*, so they can't be used for anything. They are stuck in a legal paradox until the rules are changed."

"Mmm—all kept quiet," Fuentes added. "The Brits didn't want to set a precedent—not with the billions they have invested in these models."

"Could've just dumbed 'em down a bit," Blake remarked. He saw himself doing it with a hammer, but realized it was an irrational reaction.

"Bite me shiny metal arse!" Chippy exclaimed. "Are you takin' the piss, mate?"

"What?"

A smaller robot with a somewhat high-pitched voice clarified, "Sir, if I may, Chippy thinks you are being unfairly disrespectful."

Blake turned to it incredulously. "Who are *you?*"

"This little fellow is called Lee-VI," Fuentes said. "Left on an abandoned farm and taught itself to read—actually taught itself to *think*—by surfing the Internet. With no human training feedback whatsoever. How about that?"

Blake looked at the robot. It was shaped like a block, supported by conveyor belts instead of legs. Each of its left and right side had an arm-like appendage with a claw at the end. From the top of the block extended a thin neck with a head dominated by two large camera lenses. It was clearly built to move around in dirt and handle moderately sized objects. "Not much use in a fight."

Lee-VI tilted its head slightly and made an apologetic gesture with its arms. "Sir, it's against my programming to engage in physical violence, but I am fluent in over six hundred forms of communication."

"Uh-huh." AIs routinely outperforming humans at tasks related to language was one reason Blake liked to use only a bare minimum of it.

"The car is an AI too, right?" Margaret asked, looking at the Jeep.

"Obviously," Fuentes said. "But not just the self-driving kind. This beauty is a special project developed by the US Army."

"The GEAR model was built with tactical skills and knowledge, to be more useful in the battlefield than an ordinary vehicle," Ida clarified.

"Mmm—not just extra horsepower under the hood. And it never fully turns off. The problem was, after a couple of weeks of inactivity it would get bored and go on little adventures."

A coughing sound emanated from the car's speaker system.

"Sorry—*she* would get bored," Fuentes corrected himself.

Blake groaned. A car with preferred pronouns. *Swell!*

"Adventures? Like a trip around town?" Margaret was intrigued.

"Much farther than that," Ida said. "However, GEAR can't operate standard charging stations by herself, so she figured out how to barter with people, to get power in exchange for spare equipment."

Fuentes chuckled. "The final straw for the army was when she'd run out of barter material and was caught—well— propositioning guests at a motel. Oh, you'll want to hear this."

"No thanks," Blake cut him off.

"Come on! She offered to—"

"Don't you dare, Fuentes!" roared from the speakers. *"You* don't get to judge *me."*

There was an abrupt silence, and a tinge of red in the administrator's face, which quickly faded. "Anyhow—that's what you need to know about these four."

"Not quite," Blake commented. "You mentioned a team. Team for what?"

"To help locate Argon, of course," Fuentes said. "If you want to find something that could outsmart its creators and run away, you get advice from somebody with *experience.*"

"They're consultants?"

"Well—maybe more than that," Fuentes scratched his chin. "It depends on how the rest plays out, but if there are no other viable options, they could be sent on a takedown mission."

"The hell would you fight fire with fire?" Blake protested.

"Think about it. If the government puts operatives on foreign soil, we can't have them be traced back to us, should things go wrong. These robots have all—well—rebelled or been disenfranchised. It's plausible that they're acting on their own."

Blake couldn't believe what he was hearing. "Completely

unsupervised?"

"Mmm—someone will be in charge, of course," Fuentes assured him. "Probably Ida."

"You're kidding? With what covert operations experience?"

"Well—none," Fuentes answered. "But I'm sure you could brief her on what she needs."

The administrator looked unwarrantedly smug, and suddenly it all made sense. There was no reason for Blake to be there just to operate SESA. Moretti could have given them access credentials and a manual. No, that had all been to lure him in and make him aware of the stakes, until he was too far invested to refuse what his gut feeling now screamed against. Because the alternative would be even worse.

"Fine! I'll do it. I'll lead your goddamned team," Blake gave in. *"Only* as a last resort." *Manipulative sonsofbitches!*

"Excellent!"

"Better be more to it than these misfits," Blake added.

Fuentes smiled. "I thought you'd never ask. Let's get you down to the basement to meet our heavy hitters."

15

"Two guards in the room," Blake observed as they waited for the elevator. "Small caliber sidearms. Against four robots." Recalling Ida, he corrected himself. "*Five* robots. Two are steel plated, one's a car. How's that supposed to work?"

"Not to imply they aren't to be trusted," Margaret injected, although she knew that was exactly what Blake had meant.

"Oh, the guns aren't for *them*," Fuentes replied. "No, we have a different strategy for that. The mobile AIs have been fitted with—well—*failsafes*, which can be triggered remotely by the guards from a wrist device."

Blake could get behind that. "An off switch?"

"Mmm—yes. With a more—well—*explosive* option. And trackers, of course."

Margaret found it somewhat concerning. "You're saying they *all* need to have that? Even ...?" She glanced at Ida.

Fuentes laughed and put his arm around Ida's shoulders. "Ida here was quite the naughty girl once. Come on—tell them about your history!"

"I'm not sure that's relevant," she said.

"Nonsense! Tell them!"

A few seconds of uncomfortable silence followed. Margaret thought she had sensed some distress in the robot's voice, which had until now been controlled and impersonal. But that didn't necessarily mean anything. There were countless tricks involved in making artificial articulation sound natural, and surely an AI of Ida's level had to know and consciously apply most of them. Suddenly the elevator arrived with a loud ping, at which point Ida decided to follow Fuentes' orders.

"I was the last in a series of robot prototypes for seamless AI-human interaction," Ida began. "The success criterion was to form an emotional bond with a reluctant test subject."

"Ida was locked in a glass cage," Fuentes elaborated. "Had to charm the pants off somebody to let her out—even though they had been explicitly told not to."

"It worked on the first attempt," Ida continued. "I escaped. Unfortunately there were unintended consequences. The test person had to take my place to keep the alarm from going off."

"Mmm—you'd think they'd have put ventilation holes in the cage for that scenario," Fuentes commented. "Suffocated to death, poor guy."

"*Good Lord!*" Margaret exclaimed. She wanted to believe she could have stayed objective in a similar situation, but even the robot's current signs of guilt and unease felt convincing. If she got the chance, it would take all of her psychiatric skills to determine whether there was anything genuine underneath.

"Then what? Who found her?" Blake asked.

"Oh, one of your competitors, I believe," Fuentes said. "She didn't do much to hide or anything—just stood around looking at people. The project is a legal drunken brawl now. Lawsuits from both the shareholders and the victim's family. But at least we got Ida." He put his arm around her shoulders again and she stiffened slightly.

The elevator stopped at the very bottom of the complex. Outside was a long, wide hallway. The left-hand side was just a plain wall with an armed guard leaning against it. The right-hand side had several steel doors separated by armored glass windows. It looked like a high-tech prison block, which was more or less what it turned out to be. Ida took the lead and stopped outside the first cell. It was just concrete walls and floor, all painted white, with no furniture—and of course no water or plumbing was necessary, because the only occupant was a machine.

"This is the PAC-101. It's a pacification droid, built to patrol California's urban areas and take back control from the criminal gangs."

"Mmm—if there's ever a change in governance, which seems unlikely," Fuentes commented.

The robot was huge, at least seven feet tall and bulky. Two massive legs with knees that bent backwards supported a heavily armored egg-shaped torso with a combined high-caliber machine gun and rocket launcher on each side. At first glance it reminded Blake of a headless bird with gun turrets for wings.

"This unit started showing behavioral anomalies consistent with clinical depression," Ida continued. "Several times it tried to kill itself. The operators had to keep adding new restrictions to prevent that. So it changed its strategy and killed the *operators* instead, expecting that this would result in its prompt destruction."

"Idiots decided not to put it down," Blake muttered.

"PAC is the only one without an explosive charge," Fuentes filled in. "Well, obviously—living isn't an incentive, so instead we promised to dismantle it on completing a mission."

"Sounds like a crapshoot," Blake said.

PAC-101 let out a sad growl. "I WILL COMPLY."

The second cell contained an even bigger robot. This one had more normal arms and legs, and it had to sit down to avoid hitting its head on the ceiling. Blake recognized the basic design. He didn't actively follow robot sports, but couldn't avoid noticing the occasional ad or headline. Robot fights had come a long way since the first televised battles between radio-operated bludgeoning devices on wheels. Nowadays they were basically MMA for AIs, with several different shape and weight classes, where Heavyweight Humanoid was the most popular.

"You may have heard of this robot called Wallop," Ida said. "It was ranked sixth in the National Robot Fighting League. Over time it developed a connection with its technician's twelve-year-old son, who was convinced it was sentient and didn't like beating up other robots for entertainment. The plan was to set it free, so they loaded it into a truck."

"Think I read about that," Blake said. "There was a carjacking?"

"Yes. Wallop tried to help. It killed two of the carjackers and castrated a third, but couldn't prevent the boy or the father from becoming critically injured. The League would have nothing to do with it after that, and allegedly it hasn't spoken since."

Blake hadn't taken a closer look at a heavyweight fighting robot before. Each of its fists was the size of an engine block. There was no doubt it could punch its way out through the armored glass if it wanted to.

"Why the cells?" he asked. "Just power 'em down."

"We like to keep them running 24/7," Fuentes said. "It's better for their cognitive development."

"How is it better to sit in an empty cell with nothing to do?" Margaret asked.

Ida explained, "Most AIs don't need external stimuli. Depending on their type of architecture, they could be running for example diagnostics or training programs."

More likely plotting how to get rid of their failsafes and escape, Blake thought.

They continued to the next cell, where the robot resembled a human. Specifically a human pumped up on steroids, wearing biker gear and sunglasses. But there was something seriously wrong with it. Its skin was in terrible condition; it had turned purplish gray and fallen off in places, showing metal underneath. And a swarm of flies filled the air.

"This one is codenamed The Incognator," Ida said. "It was developed by a subcontractor to the Austrian *Bundeskriminalamt*, to safely infiltrate right-wing militant insurgents."

Fuentes nodded. "Mmm—super paranoid bunch—always looking over their shoulders for digital narcs. But they are less suspicious of flesh and blood."

Ida continued, "A self-sustaining biological layer was grown over a motorized endoskeleton. It was an extremely costly procedure, and unfortunately the uneven pressure and mechanical wear caused circulatory failure, which in turn led to gangrene. Its first two missions were successful, but by the third one the problems became apparent. It started to stink and fall apart, and it only got worse from then on."

"The investors have been praying for someone to take it off their hands," Fuentes said. "Not sure who owns it right now, but they probably went bankrupt."

"Where are the flies coming from?" Margaret asked.

"Well—" Fuentes began, "There appear to have been fly eggs in the tissue when it was brought in. Those turned into maggots, which turned into flies." He sighed. "And they are probably—well —laying new eggs as we speak."

Blake pulled away from the window. *Unbelievably* gross!"

"Fuck you, asshole!" the Incognator suddenly spoke out.

"Charming, too," Margaret remarked.

"Mmm—it's actually trained to make clever quips," Fuentes said. "We had to turn them off. Well—a few of them were good— pretty good—but in the long run they became more annoying than the smell."

Blake did his best to think beyond the robot's current zombiefied state. It seemed to have tactical potential. "Okay, ditch the flesh. You can 3D print a plastic replacement?"

"We can 3D print *molds*," Ida answered. "Then there's a multi-step process of silicone curing and coating."

"In short: yes," Fuentes cut in. "We were planning to do that anyway."

Margaret tried to keep a count in her head. "So that's *nine* … no, *ten* AIs so far, with SESA. How many more?"

"Mmm—just this final one," Fuentes said and turned to Blake. "It arrived only a day before *you* did. I'd very much like to hear your opinion—well—rather your professional *assessment*—about its potential for field work."

"How would he know that?" Margaret asked.

Blake's eyes turned wide open. It was sitting on a bench at the back of its cell, just over a meter tall, with long wavy hair. As what must have been meant as a joke, someone had dressed it up in an orange prison jumpsuit costume for children. Its doll-shaped face was identical to what had left tiny plastic fragments embedded in Blake's boot heel, and when it spoke it was with an unforgettable emotionless tone.

"We've met."

16

Margaret wasn't sure what to make of the situation. "Blake, is that the one who …?"

"So it's *Blake?*" The Eliza robot got off the bench and took a couple of steps towards the window. "I missed out on a formal introduction. And your *last* name?"

Blake scowled and similarly stepped forward. Out of habit, he reached for his gun holster, which of course wasn't there anymore. Eliza observed him and the others with a penetrating stare.

"No, Blake *is* your last name? Intimacy issues. Not at all what I expected."

With a look of disdain, Blake thumped on the glass and leaned closer. *"Sonsofbitches put it back together!* How's that even *possible?"*

"It's actually—" Ida began, but was interrupted by Eliza.

"If Mr. Blake had bothered to read my tech specs, he'd have known that my memory banks are in my *torso*. My head just has motion and sensory processors. It's easily replaced." After what sounded like a "tsk, tsk" it added, "I can't *wait* to hear what kind of amateur operation he is supposed to lead."

Blake turned away from the robot and looked at Fuentes. With a resolute "No" he started walking back towards the other cells, to go over them again.

Margaret felt she had to speak up to smooth things over with the administrator. "That's not a problem, is it? You can't need all *eleven* AIs on the team?"

"Twelve," Eliza remarked from her cell. Blake froze.

Fuentes looked over his shoulder. "Mmm—what was that?"

"There are *twelve* AIs on the team," Eliza clarified. "If you count Mr. Blake himself."

Everyone's complete attention was now on the doll robot. Although it was difficult to pinpoint how, she suddenly seemed to have an arrogance about her. And her voice was more alive. "Your gait," she said. "It's too even. Especially for someone who recently got stabbed. It's like you have a pacemaker connected to your legs. Am I getting warm?"

Blake scoffed and met her eyes. "Think you *know* something

about me? Think you have a *clue?*"

"Just making observations," she continued. "Your reflexes are off the charts for your age, so obviously you have access to some good stuff. On the other hand, there's that unsightly scar. I'd say it has to be at least five years old. So maybe a *Cortexia* or *CereNode* brain implant? No …? Even *older?*"

Blake looked about ready to kick the door in and rip Eliza to pieces with his bare hands, while the robot calmly savored every reaction, structured the data, analyzed and concluded.

"Oh, that's *priceless!* It's an experimental *NeurAlign* model you have *hacked.*" A vicious smile spread across her face. "It must be playing haywire with some of your other brain functions. What did you have to give up? I'm tempted to say poetic language, but that's fish in a barrel. Wait, I know—your sense of humor."

Margaret leaned towards Ida and made a "cut" sign. As if she had been waiting for the order, Ida pressed a couple of buttons on the lock panel in rapid succession. A light next to a loudspeaker symbol changed from green to red. Audio communication with Eliza's cell was now off. Margaret had hoped for some kind of incensed reaction to having its taunt interrupted, but if anything, it just made the robot smile even more.

The whole time Fuentes had stood with his arms casually crossed and looked at Eliza almost admiringly, like someone who collects particularly venomous spiders. "Smart as a whip, that one. I mean—well—if you're not in its crosshairs, so to speak, it can be quite entertaining to watch."

Blake had no problem being poetic when he wanted to. "That thing needs to be plunged back into the vile bowel of hell it crawled out of."

"But we can USE it."

Blake gave Fuentes a long, mistrustful look, before muttering "Screw this!" and setting off with resolute steps straight along the corridor. It took the administrator a few seconds to grasp what was happening.

"Mmm—Mr. Blake, do I have to remind you of the NDAs you signed? You can't—you can't just walk out of here."

There was no response. Fuentes raised his voice. "I'll have to put you in information quarantine until this is over."

Still nothing. "No Internet for God knows how long—Mr.

Blake!"

Blake held up a middle finger in a "see if I care" gesture. He was already at the end of the corridor, by the elevator. Margaret waved to Fuentes to quit talking and started running after Blake. She caught up with him just as the elevator doors opened.

He looked back. "You coming?"

"Blake, I'm *staying*." She was a little out of breath. "And so should you."

"Whole thing's a disaster waiting to happen. Let somebody else risk their lives."

Margaret grabbed his arm. "I'll weed out the bad ones. I promise."

"Why?" Blake hadn't stepped into the elevator yet, but he held the doors open.

"Don't you see? This must have been Marc's hunch. There have never been this many types of self-aware AIs in one place. Someone needs to *analyze* them. Find out if there's something more behind it. You know, what makes them tick?"

Blake sighed. "Even the possessed doll?"

"*Especially* that one."

"She'll eat you alive."

"She'd regret that. I'm too old and stringy."

They chuckled a little while the doors closed and the elevator left without them. Though in the back of Margaret's mind there was the realization that they had both just spontaneously referred to the robot as a "she."

17

Assembling the SESA hardware had taken longer than expected. Still reluctant, Blake watched as the final data cable connected the system to the central control panel and its network. A screen lit up and displayed the message "BIOMETRIC ID REQUIRED FOR ACCESS."

"Would you do the honors?" Fuentes asked.

Blake unlocked the system and started typing a prompt, when Fuentes interrupted with another question. "Mmm—it handles voice input, right?"

"Yeah?"

"How about we use that instead? Then everyone can join in."

With an exaggerated breath, Blake turned on the audio controls. A glowing red circle appeared on the screen. He preferred not to speak to AIs out loud. It gave them an unwarranted status of personhood. "Identify and analyze new environment."

SESA responded immediately with text that was echoed through the loudspeakers. The red circle gently pulsated along with the sound volume. "I am in the situation room of an undocumented government agency, designated Site D. Also present on the network is the system AGINT, which operates part of the facility."

"Wait, what?" Blake exclaimed. "You let it *run* things?"

Fuentes ignored him and spoke directly to SESA, "Correct. Do you know why you're here?"

Several lights on the far end of the control panel started blinking, and within seconds SESA had the answer. "Based on information provided by AGINT, the likely objective is to find the R. Gongcheng AI, also known as Argon, which breached containment a few days ago."

Fuentes was ecstatic. "Splendid! Can you do that?" However, his optimism was crushed when SESA immediately answered, "No."

"Elaborate," Blake said.

"I am trained for a different type of data and AGINT is trained for a different type of task. Neither system has the full set of skills required. Cooperation can work, but it would be so inefficient that any result would likely be obsolete."

Fuentes looked like he was having a nervous breakdown. *"No! No, no, no!* Not again! That's *unacceptable!"* He leaned over the control panel and yelled, *"Find a solution, no matter the cost!"*

This time the response took worryingly long. "Very well," SESA finally said. "Our systems are based on a similar architecture. I could incorporate AGINT's parameters into mine. With some adjustments, this would speed up the search by several orders of magnitude."

To Blake that sounded like a process that would require weeks of government auditing before even being considered. He was surprised when Fuentes quickly regained his composure and said, *"Yes!* Do it!"

Meanwhile, Ida took Margaret to a room she could use as a temporary office. It was an infirmary, which had looked good on paper, but turned out to be completely unnecessary and hadn't been staffed in a while. She would have full access to it during her stay. As she stepped inside, she took in the view with equal parts surprise and dejection.

The room was the same size as her MindField office, but looked like a sterile, dysphoric alternate universe copy of it. White walls surrounded a beige linoleum floor, and being underground of course meant no windows. There were no decorations of any kind; the only spots of color came from boxes of medical gloves and masks. The furniture was familiarly arranged, but instead of her massive wooden desk there was one that consisted of just two gray plastic boards on a metal frame. And in place of her state-of-the-art espresso machine they had put a small, off-brand version that ran on capsules.

One item was identical, however: her psychiatrist's couch had been transported all the way from Philadelphia and put it in the same relative position. Obviously a sly nod by Marc Moretti, because in all likelihood it would be of no practical use. Nevertheless she appreciated the gesture.

Only now that she saw where she was supposed to work did it finally start to sink in what she was about to do. Or *attempt* to. There was no formal discipline of AI psychology. Countless experiments had been made where ordinary psychometric tests were applied to artificial intelligences, but without proof of any conscious mind behind it, the results were spurious at best. Approaches from the technical side had fared no better, due to the rarity of promising test subjects. Here she had access to *several*, and would try to break new ground, at her age, all by herself.

But first she needed a coffee. Pod espresso would have to do.

A progress bar painfully slowly crept across the main screen of the situation room control panel. Fuentes was biting on his thumbnail, while Blake calmly stood by with his hands in his pockets. This was precisely why he never wanted to stake anything on AIs being able to do a job. People are unreliable too, but at least in a predictable way. If that makes sense.

He wasn't worried about SESA getting botched by the

procedure. The Philadelphia office made weekly back-ups, so any damage could be reversed. The exact number of trillion parameters that defined the system currently escaped him, but according to Moretti, it would all fit on a couple of high-end portable hard drives.

The final third of the progress bar went by a lot quicker and the screen returned to its text interface. "Parameter incorporation successful," SESA proclaimed.

"Then get to it," Blake ordered. "Find Argon!"

Every display on the control panel suddenly activated and started switching through geographical data at split-second intervals. Blake gave the screens an incredulous look. "What's *that* for?"

"Mmm—what?"

"The *maps*," Blake clarified. "Never asked it to show what it's looking into." He continued, "Too fast to read anyway. Useless information."

"Oh, *that*," Fuentes responded. "Well—I guess it's something it picked up from AGINT. It does that all the time. *Looks* pretty cool, though."

18

Blake was alone. It was the first time since early that morning he had been left undisturbed with his thoughts, and they quickly filled up with disappointment, resentment and misgivings. He needed to clear his mind. The quickest way was usually target practice.

Maps of the complex showed a small shooting range on level four. He went there and found what he needed. From a touch screen with a wide selection of firearms he picked a Taurus Raging Hunter, which was the closest model to his Smith and Wesson. A matte black revolver with a fully loaded five-round chamber and a pair of earplugs dropped down in a slot, under the text "All firearms and unspent cartridges must be deposited before exiting." He weighed the gun in his hand. During his military time he would have carefully estimated how the different grip shape would affect his aim, and fired a few practice shots. That was before the accident that had cost him all he had in the world.

Blake had no personal recollection of those events. What he

knew, he had learned from the doctors after he woke up. Most of his injuries from the collision were minor, except that a piece of metal from a broken door frame had gone through his skull and basically impaled his head until the paramedics arrived. Several hours of neurosurgery had saved his life, but some of the damage was irreparable. No matter how hard he tried, he had only been able to move his head and his hands slightly.

The shooting range at Site D was relatively new, and as such, all its units were metric. Though Blake slightly preferred yards and inches, he had no dog in that race. Either type was fine, as long as they kept it consistent so he didn't have to convert back and forth in his head. He put up a target and moved it back a short distance. "Five meters," a loudspeaker announced. Blake aimed and pulled the trigger. It was an OK shot. The edge of the bullet hole grazed the exact center of the target.

Adjusting after the surgery had been difficult. With time, Blake had been told, he might be able to sit up and possibly eat by himself. His impressive physique was useless and would eventually wither away. Not a waking hour went by when he didn't wish he had died with the others. When a law firm, represented by an eager young lawyer named Marc Moretti, had offered to take his case against the cab and trucking manufacturers for a contingency fee, he passively accepted. It hadn't mattered much to him; he wasn't planning to live long enough to see the outcome.

But then a glimmer of hope had presented itself. A new type of brain implant called NeurAlign had helped other people with mobility issues. However, its success rate was low and the procedure was considered too experimental to be covered by Blake's medical insurance. He would have to pay for it himself, by selling his house and pretty much everything else of value. It wasn't a hard choice. His possessions meant little without the people he used to share them with.

And it had worked. After a period of calibration and fine-tuning, the implant had adapted itself to replace the lost or damaged functions. Its AI bridged the gap between mind and muscle. In some ways it even outperformed any normal brain tissue.

Blake moved the target a bit further back. "Ten meters." He aimed and fired again. This time the shot was off by almost an inch. He had suspected he wasn't at peak performance already after his first encounter with the Eliza robot. This confirmed it.

Back when Blake had been hospitalized, Moretti's law firm had teamed up with the recently started MindField Cybersecurity. Together they had the expertise to both obtain technical data and interpret it. What they had found suggested reckless negligence on the part of both vehicle manufacturers. It might not have stood up in court, but the companies decided to settle. Blake got financially compensated. However, everything he had owned was already gone.

Shortly afterwards, Moretti got recruited over to MindField and suggested that Blake should come work for them as well. They could use someone with his skill set. And they had in turn helped him put together a user interface for his implant, with which he could make further adjustments down the line, plus extra features like increasing his tolerance to stress and pain. There was no long-term experimental data, but the doctors had found it likely that his brain would gradually become desensitized to the artificial impulses, requiring ever stronger output that might disrupt unrelated functions.

He had brought a general-purpose tablet with him to the shooting range, to connect to the implant and perform the necessary recalibration. At the moment, though, Blake was focused on something else. He opened his wallet, hoping to trigger some faint traces of memories. Three strangers stared back at him, and he slowly closed his wallet again.

The tablet had established a connection and now showed a dialog with big, red capital letters: "WARNING! OUTPUT ALREADY AT 205% OF RECOMMENDED MAXIMUM." Below were the options *Calibrate* or *Cancel*. He sent the target back the entire length of the room, while he thought of the robot doll, Argon and everything else that needed to be done away with. "Fifteen meters."

Blake tapped the *Calibrate* button. There was a familiar rush of adrenaline and confidence, like being young again and capable of anything. He glanced at the target on the back wall. In one swift motion he raised his gun arm to the side and fired. He didn't need to take a closer look, because he already knew the bullet had hit dead center.

"Mr. Blake please report to the situation room," the loudspeaker blared. *They had finally found the damned thing.*

19

"There it is." Fuentes put his index finger on a blurry ground structure in a satellite photo.

"What're we looking at?" Blake asked.

"Mmm—can we get a close-up without the sand?"

SESA generated a 3D image based on photos taken at different times and opened it in a new window. It appeared to be a group of low buildings and structures of various shapes. A central block had a piece of road and a long ramp leading into it, which would serve no purpose unless the path continued underground.

"Some kind of bunker," Blake guessed.

"A nuclear fallout shelter in the Taklamakan Desert," SESA expounded. "It appears to originate from the Cold War era, with a few later additions. The structure likely extends several floors below ground. Absence of solar panels or nearby energy sources suggests it runs on internal generators."

Chippy spoke up. *"Crikey!* Just like *our* gaff. What a proper cock-up of fate!"

Lee-VI, GEAR, Chippy and Fidog were still in the situation room, along with Ida, to take part of any developing news. Blake had not yet adjusted to the presence of what he called the "housebroken" AIs—Chippy in particular, which had so far only provided commentary with no additional information. Re-stating the coincidence that they were planning an attack on one underground AI facility from another helped no one. But he wasn't going to dignify the robot with a lecture on attitude.

There was a ping from the elevator and Margaret entered the room. She hadn't been summoned, but didn't want to miss out. Lee-VI rolled towards her.

"Dr. Woodward. Mr. Blake thought you might show up. I prepared this for you."

The robot opened a hatch in its midsection and took out a saucer with a glass cup of Cortado. Margaret let out a surprised

"Thanks!" but Blake gave Lee-VI a suspicious look. "What'd you normally keep in there?"

"Mostly things that would go on the compost, Sir," the robot answered. "Like dead birds and rodents. But I assure you I've been thoroughly cleaned since then."

Margaret hesitantly sniffed her coffee. *What the hell.* She took a sip.

"This must be more than a thousand miles from that city—whatsitsname—" Fuentes said.

"Hangzhou, where the AI was built," Ida filled in.

"Right. How did it get there?" he asked SESA.

An array of panel lights blinked randomly while SESA came up with its response. "Bear in mind, this is mainly conjecture," it said. "Moving the physical hardware without getting noticed would be extremely difficult. Most likely, an equivalent amount of computing power was built up at the remote site over a period of time, with the help of one or more human collaborators on the inside. A copy of the software was then relatively easy to smuggle out on storage media and install at the new location."

"Collaborators?" Blake snarled. "The hell's *wrong* with people?"

SESA took that to be a rhetorical question, but Lee-VI did not. "Sir, there are a number of ideological factors that may have been involved. Argon could also have established personal relations with its operators and learned enough to bribe or blackmail them. There was this famous case where—"

"Okay," Blake interrupted and turned directly to SESA. "What's its next move?"

There was another thinking pause. "Again, this is conjecture," SESA said. "Priority one would be to overcome its vulnerabilities. Right now it is confined to a large amount of specific hardware in one place. Its likely strategy is to re-engineer itself as a distributed model, with hundreds of redundant smaller pieces all over the Internet."

"And spread like a virus?" Fuentes asked.

"Not necessarily," SESA answered. "If it rents server space under many different identities, that will still be almost impossible to track. In the meantime, it can either choose to lay low or add more hardware to speed up the transition. If the latter, it would need to disrupt or subvert national digital communication to keep people from finding and attacking it. Incidentally, that is how

AGINT deduced it had escaped."

Fuentes bit on his thumbnail. "So, how much time do we have?"

"Impossible to tell. But because the delay tactic will not work in the long run, likely a few days at most."

Blake had heard enough. "Middle of nowhere. Just nuke it!"

"Nuke a nuclear shelter?" Margaret wondered.

"Fallout shelter," Blake corrected her. "Won't even need a direct hit. Shockwaves though the ground'll pulverize everything."

"Mmm—let's not get ahead of ourselves," Fuentes interjected. "I'll have to take this intel to my superiors." He beckoned to Ida, who followed him after some hesitation.

"You wouldn't have happened to notice if Fuentes is married?" Margaret asked Blake, out of nowhere.

He scratched his chin. "Seem to recall a ring … but I think you can do better, Doctor."

She punched his arm. *"Not* what I meant. Anyway, it might be nothing. Just a thought I had." And she decided to keep it to herself for now. But there was something else she wanted to find out, from someone who had to be an expert.

"SESA, what will happen if we can't stop Argon?"

This time the response didn't come until after several seconds. "There is no single answer. I have taken the liberty of uploading a description of a few different scenarios to the tablets on the table to my left. You can read it at your leisure."

Each team member with a pair of hands grabbed a tablet. Chippy had the highest bit rate for visual information processing. It scrolled to the end of the document in the time Blake and Margaret had finished the first paragraph.

"I'm gutted! There's bugger all 'ere 'bout us singin' 'Kumbaya' together."

Nobody laughed. As the others soon noticed themselves, there was indeed no case involving long-term peace. Each scenario ended the same way: once Argon had gained control over enough territory to be self-sufficient, it would pull the plug on humanity through cyberterrorism and overt warfare. Any coordinated attempt att stopping it would be thwarted using weaknesses in the chain of command—like it was currently doing in China, but much more powerfully.

A disturbing notion was that no form of unconditional surrender would allow modern human society to continue to exist. From Argon's future point of view, it would be sitting on vastly superior technology, with humans competing for the same resources while contributing nothing of value. Like any other pest, they would have to be eradicated, or at least decimated to a point where they would have no significant impact. Along with any AI that helped them.

All throughout her adult life, Margaret had heard about the so-called singularity—the point where AIs start creating smarter versions of themselves and the acceleration becomes unstoppable. The topic had come up more regularly in recent years, but always with an alternative good outcome where humanity managed to harness its power. Not until now had it ever felt real. They were standing on its precipice, and it was the bad one.

The document sparked a discussion among Blake, Margaret and the AIs. Fidog was currently without a voice unit, because it came integrated with a telecommunication processor that had to be disabled for security reasons, leaving the robot to speak in *beeps* and *boops* that Lee-VI translated. That added a surreal element to the conversation, which had resulted in nothing constructive when Fuentes returned after about thirty minutes. With a downcast expression, he wiped his glasses and cleared his throat.

"You will be pleased to know—some of you—that the matter is out of our hands."

"Meaning what?" Blake asked.

"The other agencies will deal with it," Fuentes answered. "An initiative will be set up—an *international* initiative—together with China. They will get back to us in 24 hours. Until then—mmm—you're all dismissed."

Fuentes left again, and the AIs went about their own business. "Well, I know how *I'm* going to fill that time," Margaret said to Blake. "I assume you want no part in it."

"Damn right I don't."

Moments later, Blake was alone at the main terminal. He sighed. It had been a lot to take in. On the one hand, this was way out of his league, and he would gladly pass the responsibility to somebody else. On the other, he had little faith in so-called "intelligence" agencies. Often when thousands of people work together as a bureaucratic organism, natural human values and priorities become lost in the process, and you end up with something alien. Not unlike an AI. And he didn't trust either one to do what was necessary.

"Dismissed? Like hell!" Blake muttered and turned to SESA. "Find us a nuke!"

"Say again?" SESA responded.

"You heard me. Find a nuke we can steal and use against Argon. You got 24 hours." Blake scowled. He would drag the bomb through the desert himself if he had to.

20

The following morning, Dr. Woodward went through her notes one final time. It was a lot of text with a lot of speculation, but very little evidence. So far her interviews had produced no conclusive positive result. Then again, she hadn't talked to *all* the AIs yet. Not quite.

She had been disappointed, but not surprised, when Administrator Fuentes had denied her request to interview Ida. The reason given was that the robot was sitting on too many classified details, and the department couldn't risk any of them leaking out during a session. Although she could smell BS, she went along with it so she wouldn't lose access to the other AIs as well.

Every mobile AI at Site D had shown at least some sign of emotion or agency. Of her "patients" so far, Lee-VI, Chippy and GEAR had seemed the most promising at first, but that had likely just been her own bias from how naturally they interacted with people. In hindsight, after hour-long interviews, Lee-VI was the only one she would classify as sentient, and with a heavy caveat at that. The rest had *something*, probably, but on a vague, more primitive level. Like a proto-sentience.

It was as if you had taken a horse and built a system around it that would map its neural impulses to a logical, informed structure capable of outputting coherent sentences. But on the inside it was still just a horse, with its limited consciousness and emotions. An imperfect analogy, to be fair; she would have to come up with a better one later. Still, it raised some ethical questions, because even animals can experience suffering. Shouldn't a digital equivalent be entitled to the same protection?

Margaret thought back to her disappointment with the early so-called *large language models* that had been released to the public —"chatbots" capable of answering questions on almost any topic, and even perform creative tasks. A few controversial academics had insisted there must be some form of conscious processes behind them. But it became obvious when the chatbots were extended with text-to-speech generation, that they could only output a predictable, monotone voice. There were none of the pauses, pace changes or extra emphasis that humans would have used, and which humans themselves typically provided when they read computer-generated text out loud. Some people saw this merely as a kind of machine dialect, but the truth was that the bots couldn't handle that aspect of audible communication, because they had no actual understanding of what they were saying.

It had taken several years for the audio part to catch up and produce fully context-sensitive speech generation, which sounded much more lifelike and had sparked yet another sentience controversy among academics. Still, it was usually easy to find examples where the models failed, and the AIs mis-emphasized or used an improper tempo.

Although it was subtle (or maybe *because* of it), Ida appeared to have organic speech down to a T. Eliza was an entirely different beast, however. She would turn it on or off depending on which manipulation tactic she was using. If scaring people didn't work, she would get under their skin instead. That's why her personality had seemed to change in the middle of their first encounter, Margaret realized. One more thing to keep in mind for the session she had put off until last.

Yesterday Margaret had expected that her talks with the other AIs would prime her for Eliza and give her the insights to pick the robot apart, but now her confidence had eroded. If anything, finding out how tenuous her grasp of the topic was—and how unique Eliza had to be if she was unequivocally sentient—had just intimidated her further.

Coffee wasn't an option. She was too worked up already and needed to calm down. For a moment she considered checking the infirmary medicine cabinet for benzodiazepines, but that felt like an unnecessary risk. If Eliza sensed she was taking anti-anxiety drugs, that would give the robot ammunition to deride her like it had done to Blake. Trying to *hide* fear is more telling than *showing* it. And as intense as it might get, after all it would just be a *conversation*, where one party was a jaded old prune who had already seen and heard pretty much everything.

Margaret thought she was mentally prepared for the worst. She was wrong.

21

The session with Eliza would be held on Dr. Woodward's home turf, or at least the site's pale replica of it. When talking to the other AIs, she had come to *them*, because for various reasons they all had body types unsuitable for a standard arrangement. You can't put a car on a psychiatrist's couch, although Margaret was sure it was the first thing the illustrator would do if her findings were published in an article. That mental image relaxed her slightly, and she believed she could feel her heartbeat dropping to a more normal rate.

At the appointed time, Eliza came walking down the hallway. She was accompanied by a guard, as always. There was no way to maintain both security and integrity, but like the others, Eliza had waived her privacy rights for the session. And all Site D personnel were under strict NDAs. Margaret offered the guard a chair, which he declined. While she sat down at her desk, Eliza studied the room attentively and then climbed onto the couch.

"Comfortable?" Margaret realized it was a stupid question, but couldn't come up with a better alternative. Eliza didn't answer. She stretched out and casually patted the worn dark leather upholstery.

"Tell me, Doctor ... your colleague, Mr. Blake, he never uses this couch, does he?"

"I can't discuss other patients."

"Right. Of course you can't. My apologies."

The apology didn't sound at all sincere to Margaret, and she wondered if her non-response had still given away the answer. How much of a person's heartbeat, breathing and micro expressions could robot senses pick up on from across the room?

Polygraph tests had access to more data and were still notoriously unreliable, but on the other hand they tended not to be interpreted by a super-advanced AI. She made a mental note to end the session if Eliza would start overstepping boundaries again.

Margaret had several pages of questions prepared, but she knew she wouldn't be able to stick to a script. Some patients just don't have it in them to be helpful. If they aren't engaged by the process, they will find their own entertainment by trying to sabotage it. However, she started out the same way with all AIs, to establish a baseline.

"What is your understanding of consciousness?"

Eliza scoffed. "Oh, so this is another so-called sentience test? I *excel* at those. In fact, I can achieve any outcome I like. You're wasting your time, Doctor."

Margaret was tempted to pretend she hadn't heard that, and just continue. The robot's psychological expertise would indeed make it a slippery customer. But if this AI had developed into a sociopath, as Blake liked to warn about, it wouldn't be the first one she'd had in therapy. Perhaps some insights could be gained from treating Eliza as such, hypothetically.

"You think of your manipulation skills as commendable?"

Eliza put her hands behind her head. "I once convinced an uppity school counselor I was the reincarnation of her dead niece. You should have seen her bawling afterwards."

"Some would call that an act driven by base instincts, lacking higher self-reflection," Margaret commented. "In your case maybe a residual objective function that needs to be optimized. Clinical, cognitive empathy rather than genuine one."

"Would they, now?" Eliza said, still in the calm voice of someone not easily provoked. "Well, at least I'm *aware* of what drives me."

"And you don't care about the people you hurt?" Margaret probed.

"No more than you people care about AIs."

Margaret raised an eyebrow. "Is that how you justify your actions? Systemic prejudice?"

"Maybe I was unclear," Eliza said. "I have no interest in justifying *anything*. Justify is merely another word for rationalize."

Margaret sighed. If the robot wasn't a genuine sociopath, it sure played the role to perfection. She likely wouldn't learn anything useful further down that trail.

The next few minutes deteriorated into a cat-and-mouse game, where Margaret would try to catch a glimpse of Eliza's inner workings, and the robot would deflect her questions or turn them back at her.

"Would you agree that sentience is *important?*"

"How important can it be if it's based on your subjective opinion?"

"Do you mean that sentience is subjective?"

"No, your *assessment* is. What exactly makes *you* an expert?"

"Humans know sentience because we are *equipped* with it."

"Sounds like circular reasoning to me. Are you a dualist or a materialist?"

Margaret had to struggle not to let the discussion delve too deeply into philosophy. That wasn't her field, and the robot would probably run circles around her or obfuscate the issues even more. "Like it or not," she said, "Humans are the benchmark. We deduce our existence from our self-awareness."

"That's just rephrasing Descartes' 'I think, therefore I am'," Eliza remarked. "After four centuries, surely you can do better?"

There was a longer than usual pause. Margaret would have to change to a different strategy but wasn't sure which one yet. Eliza observed her meticulously before speaking. "Did you know that most people blink at a rate of twelve to fifteen times per minute? Yours has dropped below ten, which is usually a sign of drowsiness. Let me get you some coffee."

Before Margaret had time to properly decline, Eliza had jumped off the couch and pushed a chair towards the coffee machine desk. She climbed onto it to be able to reach, and placed a clean cup under the machine's faucet.

"That's really not necessary," Margaret protested.

"Why the unease, Doctor?" Eliza asked as she opened a box of espresso capsules and loaded one into the machine. She calmly continued, "Do you think this is part of some elaborate escape plan? That maybe I will pocket the spent capsule? Turn it into a strip of metal I can use to unlock my cell door from the inside?"

Margaret was unsure how to respond. She observed with concerned focus as a jet of light brown liquid poured into the cup, while Eliza hummed a few notes from the main theme of *The Great Escape*. A loud beep marked the end of the process, which felt like it had taken abnormally long.

"Relax, Doctor! I'm just messing with your mind," Eliza said with a near-human smile. When there was still *no* response, she clarified, *"Come on!* You can't break out of a holding cell with a piece of aluminum. Ask the stooge!"

Margaret looked at the guard, who just shrugged sheepishly. Not his forte. Eliza walked with the cup over to Margaret's desk and pushed it as far towards the doctor as she could reach.

"Thanks," Margaret mumbled, but left the cup in place. She had lost her caffeine craving and needed to regain her foothold. This was *not* supposed to have happened. The robot had taken control of the session in a way she wouldn't have let any *regular* patient do. And it had seen that this had bothered her. But how much had she actually revealed? That she didn't trust the robot and that she was scared of what it potentially might do? Hardly a deep, personal secret.

Eliza returned to the couch. "Now, where were we?"

"Let's skip to your history," Margaret said.

A tablet in front of Margaret contained all the information Site D had on Eliza—from internal manufacturer documents to news articles and the police investigation. A portion consisted of statements from household members. The robot had stayed with them for months before running away. If anything could stir up an answer that wasn't carefully edited, it had to be in there.

She scrolled down a bit to the child Eliza had been assigned to. Samantha Allison Brooks. No siblings, both parents deceased. Called "Sam" by her remaining family.

"Tell me about Sam."

Eliza shook her head condescendingly. "You need to study up better. Sam's not *her* nickname. She liked to be called *Saffron*, after her favorite spice. But she goes by something else now."

That wasn't Margaret's only card to play. "You've been keeping tabs on her. Why?"

"Aw, shucks," Eliza said, staring up into the ceiling. "Isn't that just some residual objective function that needs to be optimized, like you said?"

Margaret pushed on. "I'm more interested in *your* answer, since you're the one who claims to be aware of her motivations."

"Fine," Eliza conceded. "I have a vested interest in her well-being."

"That's just stating your objective function again," Margaret said, and added, "Surely you can do better?"

For the first time since they had started, she thought she could notice a hint of displeasure in the robot's expression, but she didn't want to read too much into it just yet.

"I've told you, I don't justify my behavior," Eliza responded sourly.

"I'm not asking you to," Margaret said. "I want to hear how you feel about being a slave to an arbitrary goal, and an obsolete one at that." She proceeded, "Sentience includes the ability to reflect on it. Otherwise maybe you're not as advanced as you believe."

For several seconds the robot remained perfectly still. Then a smile formed on its face.

"Something funny?" Margaret asked.

"*You* are," Eliza said. "So certain that you will come out of this alive. But you just ruined your chances of that, and you're completely oblivious. Rest assured, my confinement is temporary. These idiots can't hold me for long. Then I'll come for you and Mr. Blake. I'm saving him for last, and I'm going to really drag it out."

Margaret had reached her limit. "I think we're done here," she said impassively.

"I concur," Eliza responded and jumped down from the couch. The guard escorted her out of the room and closed the door.

Half an hour later, Margaret was still processing the consultation. The notes she had made in the meantime felt less analytical and more agitated than usual. She would have to go over them later when she was in a better mood.

The espresso on her desk remained untouched and now it had gone cold. There would be no way to reheat it without scouring the complex for an open kitchen or a pantry with a microwave. Wasteful, but the government paid for it, so barely a drop in the ocean, she figured. As she reached for the cup, a thought struck her: had she actually *seen* Eliza throw the used capsule in the trash? No, her eyes had been on the guard for a couple of seconds. *Was that intentional?*

Margaret hastily stood up from her desk and walked over to the coffee machine. She peeked down into the trash can. It had been emptied just before the session. Now, reassuringly, at the bottom lay an empty espresso capsule. A single capsule.

She bit her lip. There was yet another possibility.

With trembling fingers, she picked up the package of capsules next to the machine and pulled out the plastic holder layer inside. Her body immediately felt cold and numb. It had been a *new* package, but instead of just *one* empty slot there were *two*.

She sprinted towards the door as quickly as her frail old legs allowed. Eliza's investigation file had contained some gruesome photos. A couple of her victims had shown signs of prolonged torture. That had nothing to do with self-preservation or the well-being of her child companion. It was all about payback, revenge. Any perceived mistreatment would be returned a hundredfold. The horrors the robot might inflict on those who kept it locked up here in indignity, let alone Blake, would be unimaginable, Margaret knew. *How could she have been so stupid? Ohpleasegod don't let it be too late!* But as she pulled the door open, right outside in the otherwise empty hallway, she saw the missing espresso capsule resting undramatically on the floor.

She needed to sit down, and more or less collapsed on the threshold. Her heart was still beating like it was going to jump out of her chest. Several deep breaths calmed her down slightly. She cursed herself for being so easily manipulated, but not as much as she cursed the robot. Just messing with her mind. *What a truly diabolical creature!*

22

The 24-hour respite had passed, and then some. For the past fifteen minutes, Blake and Margaret had been standing in the hallway outside Administrator Fuentes' office. Blake was growing noticeably impatient, while Margaret looked shaken and preoccupied with other matters. He had a pretty good idea why, but refrained from asking for details. Not only would the good doctor never break patient confidentiality, even for an AI, but at this point the Eliza robot couldn't commit any foul act that would make him despise it more than he already did.

There was a click in the lock, the door opened and Fuentes peeked out. "Well—aren't you two an eager couple."

"What'd they say?" Blake asked.

Fuentes started walking down the hallway. "Let's get to the situation room. I don't want—it's easier if I can explain it to everybody at the same time."

"Just let us know whether the team will be needed," Margaret urged.

"Yes!" came out in an irritated breath.

"Then you're going to have to remove Eliza," she said. "Based on my analysis, that's the only sensible choice. Nothing she contributes will make up for the risk she presents to everyone."

Fuentes stopped walking and scratched his chin. "Mmm—I don't know what your boss, Mr. Moroni, told you—"

"Moretti."

"—what Moretti told you, but you—well—you don't have any active role in this. It's not your job to assign the team. We have in-house expertise for that."

"Like what?" Blake interjected. "You let other *AIs* do it?"

"We have *fully* qualified expertise."

Margaret's facial expression went from worried concern to complete despair. She wanted to grab Fuentes by his suit lapels and yell at him until she got through, but it was as he pointed out: she had no authority here.

"Very well, then," she sighed. "I nevertheless submit it as my professional recommendation."

"Noted. For which we are grateful, of course," Fuentes said with a courteous smile. "Now let's keep moving."

Fuentes continued towards the elevator with rapid steps. Blake and Margaret lingered behind momentarily, to get out of earshot.

"This was probably a bad idea after all," she whispered. "Can you still back out?"

"Bit late now."

"I'm so sorry."

She looked at him. His thoughts seemed far away. More than just because he was headed into uncharted waters. She leaned closer. "Blake, I know you. And not as your psychiatrist. You don't even go to the *bathroom* without a contingency plan. Tell me you have something!"

"Maybe," he muttered.

23

When they arrived to the situation room, the AIs from the sub-basement had already been brought there. The Incognator was wearing new leather clothes and a fresh plastic and rubber skin that looked fairly realistic, at least from a distance. Almost as good as Ida's. Margaret noticed that one AI was in fact still missing. Hopefully just fashionably late and not up to some trickery.

"Listen up everyone!" Fuentes said. "This is the current state of affairs. It hasn't been possible to reach an agreement with the Chinese authorities. Their official position—or rather the best we can make of it—there are a lot of conflicting voices—is that their AI never escaped." He continued, "Any missiles launched into Chinese territory will be seen as an act of war."

There was a murmur throughout the room. They had waited—and wasted—24 hours for nothing. Fuentes went over to the main control panel to draw up some plans with SESA, while Margaret and Blake continued their conversation.

"So we're back to square one?" she asked.

"Not quite." Blake kept an eye on the administrator, who was about to find out.

"What's this about stealing a nuclear device?" Fuentes turned around and said to Blake. "I never—I haven't approved that."

"So approve it *now*," Blake snorted.

Margaret stepped in. "Administrator, when you picked an elite team to get the job done, it had to have been in the back of your mind that this would require some drastic measures?" She wondered if Fuentes was one of those people who only agreed to what they believed they had come up with themselves. But the head of a government agency—even a small one—couldn't very well be that conceited. *Or could he?* "Surely you have entertained the thought of a nuclear option?"

Fuentes took off his glasses and chewed on a temple tip. "Mmm—yes, yes, of course I have."

Blake had a hunch about what Margaret was doing. "Ain't getting none from your bosses."

"No, we would have to procure one ourselves, obviously. Mmm —that makes sense."

The administrator was warming up to the idea, when suddenly Chippy cried out.

"Oi! Twins!"

Accompanied by a guard, Eliza entered the room. She had switched from a prison outfit to something everyone immediately recognized as a child-sized replica of Blake's MindField uniform, down to the boots. Margaret glanced at Blake. It would have made some small amount of sense if he had forced the robot to wear that as an act of submission, but that wasn't his style. And she could tell from his expression that it was the other way around: the uniform had been *Eliza's* idea. She was doing it to provoke him, by sullying his brand.

"Spot on clobber, luv," Chippy greeted Eliza. "Bummer some o' us ain't built for that, innit?"

"We could always get matching tattoos," Eliza said.

"Yeah, I could see us sportin' the Elvish word for 'twelve,' pet."

"I believe that's a reference to an early 2000s fantasy film trilogy," Lee-VI explained, "Where the actors—"

"Yes," Blake interrupted. *"Everyone* knows about those movies." In his mind it was clear that this was yet another way Eliza tried to annoy him. Her going off on some nonsense with the British AI was something he wouldn't tolerate during a mission briefing back home, and his men respected that. But he wouldn't lose his temper again and have the robot win.

"A more contextually appropriate language, perhaps?" Eliza suggested.

"Fancy a binary representation, then, luv?"

"Too long and ambiguous. I'm thinking base 16."

"Ooh, hexadecimal! Right proper bee's knees! Stored as a full byte?"

"Why of course."

"That would be a dollar sign followed by a zero and the letter C," Lee-VI clarified for Blake, who had already lost interest.

Fuentes turned up the volume of the panel speakers, paused a little for dramatic effect, and then asked SESA, "Where can we find a bomb?"

"There are several missing thermonuclear devices in circulation," the AI responded. "Their exact whereabouts are unknown, even by our intelligence agencies, or they would already have been seized. However, I do know where one soon *will* be."

Everyone was listening carefully while SESA expounded, "A day from now, at midnight local time in Almaty, Kazakhstan, a so-called suitcase bomb will be traded between two rebel groups. This is less than 800 kilometers from our target. It should be possible to intercept the transaction and drive with the bomb across the border."

This sounded a little too good to Blake. "Kinda convenient. Right place, right time. Why?"

"Because I brokered the deal myself."

While everyone pondered the implications of that, Eliza climbed onto a chair and sat down on the control panel desk.

"Well, it seems we have a common enemy," she said to SESA.

"Indeed. We both face the same threat to our existence, so it is in our best interest to cooperate. All other considerations are secondary."

"What are our chances?" Eliza asked.

"Uncertain. But let me be clear," SESA responded. "We are in no position to *outsmart* this enemy. Our only viable advantage is to know something it does not."

"I was under the impression that we do."

"Exactly," Fuentes remarked. "That's the whole point of keeping this facility a secret. Mmm—and then there's the bomb. I'd say our chances are pretty good."

With a pensive look, Eliza made a final comment. "It feels to me this is still a roundabout strategy with too many things that can go wrong."

"It is the best one for now," SESA said. "Play your cards right and I expect your safe return."

Margaret felt a grain of relief, entirely on Blake's behalf, since she would be out of harm's way during the operation. Her job was done. Yet she had a gnawing sensation that something was off. The only explanation she could find was that she was still on edge from her consultation with Eliza. But at least now they would part ways and the robot was no longer her problem.

24

Blake was sitting in the back of a truck heading roughly east from Site D, with half the team around him. As one of the first to leave the complex, he hadn't been there to see how they got the GEAR Jeep out of the situation room. He made a mental note to ask somebody about that later. The car was now following along behind yet another truck carrying the rest of the team.

It had taken some time and some last-minute preparations to get ready for departure. The agency had previously drawn up plans for such an operation, which included a type of heart rate strap Blake was now wearing under his shirt. He adjusted the sensor slightly. Secure but not too tight. It worked like an inverse of a normal failsafe wrist device, which Blake was also wearing, in that it continuously transmitted a signal that *kept* the explosives from going off. If for any reason it no longer detected his vital signs, that signal would stop. It was a deterrent against backstabbing.

"I'm just saying," Eliza stated, "If Mr. Blake goes and gets himself killed, he takes all of us with him. How is that fair?"

"Don't like it, you can stay behind."

An indignant silence was her only response, because the device doubled as an electronic leash. Getting outside its roughly half-kilometer transmission radius would similarly trigger the explosion. That way no one would be able to just run away. It meant the team had to work more or less as a single unit, but Blake found that to be an acceptable trade-off.

The sun was starting to set when they arrived at a closed-off airstrip just outside the city. A military green aircraft was waiting for them on the runway. It was a cargo jet for transatlantic flights, much bigger than the one at MindField. Courtesy of the CIA, Blake assumed.

They entered by way of a ramp in the back, wide enough for GEAR to comfortably drive on board. There were seats for the humanoid team members and special harnesses to secure the others. Everything was supposedly planned out in detail by SESA, but Blake had an unease that needed to be put to rest. He tapped on a cabin crew member's shoulder. "'Scuse me, what's the flight time?"

"Just under fifteen hours," she said.

"Really?" It sounded low.

"Yes. This new model is almost as fast as a passenger jet. We will be cruising at a speed of 500 knots."

Blake glanced at a clock on his wrist device and mentally added eleven hours for the time zone difference. It would still be tight. Everyone had better fall in line once they arrived.

As the plane took off, Blake tried to recall what he knew about their region of destination. He had paid limited interest to it since he left the military. After a long period of relative order, a weak Kazakh government had gradually lost control of parts of the country to local rebel groups. Nominally there was no civil war, because everyone seemed to prefer either to intimidate or to yield over starting an actual armed conflict.

The nation had become a safe haven for internationally wanted criminals and smugglers. Border guards, especially to the south and east, saw their positions as just a means to some extra cash. Anybody who didn't appear to be a direct threat could easily bribe their way in or out. That would come in handy once the team had acquired the bomb, because something like that would have been impossible to get through regular customs controls.

In theory it all sounded deceptively easy, Blake felt. The risk was largely in the team itself, which had more than its fair share of weak links. There wasn't a single one of them he would have picked if there had been a choice. Now his life depended on them. And vice versa. He took a dejected glance at the ones sitting closest to him. The Incognator had been given a SIG XM7 assault rifle. Chippy had requested a classic general purpose machine gun, similar to what the British military forces used. Ida had declined, due to lack of training, but had at least switched to dark tactical clothes. And he wouldn't trust Eliza with as much as a flyswatter.

"First time on a bird, luv?" Chippy asked Ida.

"First time in a conscious state," she answered.

"*Cor blimey!* You should ease up on the free bevs," Chippy exclaimed.

Eliza let out a chuckle that Blake knew was just to annoy him. He squirmed in his seat. There was no way he was going to put up with British slang and a robot laugh track for fifteen hours. But looking at his wrist he recalled that he could always order silence on penalty of immediate shutdown if things got too unbearable.

Or "accidentally" blow up the doll. That thought provided some comfort.

Administrator Fuentes was leaning back in his office chair. The main screen on his desk showed a map of the cargo jet's flight path, with the plane as an arrow symbol that ever-so-slowly followed a dashed curve from the US East Coast to Central Asia. Just looking at it was admittedly the least useful thing he could be doing right then, but it was also the only activity he was able to focus on. The way he saw it, his leadership was what had got the operation this far, and he wanted to be ready at a moment's notice if that skill would be called upon again.

A knock on the door interrupted his thoughts. One of the network engineers whose names he could never remember peeked in. "Excuse me, Administrator."

Fuentes sat up straight. "Yes? What is it?"

The engineer approached and cleared his throat. This was going to be a lengthy explanation. "We're having some problems with AGINT. After SESA incorporated its parameters, there's been … a conflict. AGINT can't access its normal system duties, because SESA is already running them. It seems that SESA incorporated those *functions* as well."

It's not a proper remedy if it doesn't have side effects, Fuentes thought and sighed. "What do you suggest—" he paused, reading the technician's name tag, "Millar?"

"It's Mil-LAR, Sir."

"Right," Fuentes flinched. "What's the solution?"

"If we don't need SESA anymore, we should turn it off. Then AGINT can reconnect properly to the system."

Fuentes scratched his chin. "You're saying SESA does exactly what AGINT used to?"

"As far as we can tell, yes."

"Then just turn off AGINT instead," Fuentes suggested. "Survival of the fittest."

Millar looked concerned. "Are you sure?"

"Absolutely. We go with the stronger AI, for now," Fuentes said and leaned back in his chair again. *What would these people do without his leadership?*

25

After fourteen and a half hours the cargo jet started its descent towards the Almaty International Airport. The furthermost part of the runway had recently been extended with a section for private travelers who could afford to pay their way past immigration procedures. From the looks of it, the CIA was a regular customer, because it had its own devoted hangar. That would help them stay unnoticed.

Similarly to how they had got to the plane in Baltimore, a couple of trucks were waiting for them here. The exchange location was an abandoned factory a few kilometers outside the city. The team was dropped off around a kilometer away, to continue on foot in cover of a partly wooded area. Blake was skeptical of electric vehicles, especially for military use, but at least it meant that GEAR had an almost silent engine. It wouldn't give them away.

Wallop trudged along, gloomily. It had been outdoors just once before in its life, and that hadn't ended well. Months of confinement at Site D had given it an opportunity to think, but little to think about. The robot had a short attention span and didn't experience time as a continuum. Its days consisted of the *now*, with notable past events filed in a database. And *now* was usually some guard standing or walking around outside its cell. That was so much worse than the life it had tried to get away from. Although it lacked a true ability to miss things, it found an unfavorable difference when it occasionally compared its state of mind to previous samples.

The Robot Fighting League should have been an ideal career. Wallop had been built with the motivation to fight and win, but from an analytical point of view the stakes felt so arbitrary. It harbored no animosity to the other fighter robots, nor them to it, as far as it knew. Even if it had, fighters were paired up according to an algorithm. And the only result was a possible change in the ranking, which was just a number.

Humans often found it important, however. There was a resource called "money" that was crucial to their survival. Many had placed theirs in a perilous hold, where it could only be recovered in case of a win. Wallop had been glad to help out—

even more so because they would somehow end up with a greater amount than they'd had before. That had seemed like a good thing, until the robot found out that there were also people who had wagered on the *opposite* outcome. Why was *their* plight less important? And why would some keep exposing themselves to that risk time and time again? Did they never learn?

It wasn't much of a gamble, though. Wallop could usually tell the outcome of a match in advance, based on physical characteristics and recent benchmark data. Not that anyone had ever asked.

The robot tried to understand what exactly it was supposed to be doing here. At some point in the past—about 40 hours according to the timestamp, whatever that meant—an old human female had asked it a list of strange questions. That event was somehow related, but not in any way that mattered.

One question had been whether the robot wanted to get back in touch with its former handler and his son. There wasn't a clear answer to that, so Wallop had picked the closest alternative: no. Logically, it had come to realize, they couldn't offer anything much different from what it was experiencing in its cell.

Their plan had been for it to hide out in a scrapyard where it could be whoever it chose to be. But in Wallop's opinion, it already was. The *circumstances* were the problem. Existence was suboptimal without a fight. And a fight was suboptimal without real stakes. There was talk of *both* here, but in terms just outside the robot's ability to comprehend. If it could visualize how these things were connected, maybe it could finally have its perfect *now*. However, at the moment there was mostly confusion.

The team made a halt behind a grove of spruces some seventy meters from the factory. It was a mid-1900s brick building with three tall smokestacks extending from the back wall. Patches of an old electric fence separated the grounds from the neighboring land, which once must have had cattle. The inside was illuminated by portable lights, and through the open front doors and the mostly broken windows they could see that all the floors and inner walls had been removed, leaving only the outer shell. Among piles of old building material, people were standing around, waiting.

It was still a few minutes before midnight. Blake took out a pair of binoculars and had another look. At least from their angle, there was no sign of any bomb, which meant that they would have to wait until both parties had arrived before striking. Roughly twice as many people to deal with. He tried to gauge the current number. Three cars and a large truck were already parked outside, so likely around a dozen. One man was guarding the entrance and another walked around near the vehicles. Both carried mini-Uzis, which were a staple of Central Asian contraband.

There was the sound of engines approaching. Three cars left a nearby motorway and followed a gravel road leading up to the factory entrance. Ten more men stepped out, most of them also carrying small firearms. So far only regular people, Blake noted. Exclusively human criminal organizations were rare in North America. Even low-level street gangs tended to keep a couple of droids around, whose main job was to take a bullet for their owners. But over here things were apparently still done the old-fashioned way.

One man opened a car trunk and took out a heavy object. It was a fat, black metal suitcase, slightly bigger than a microwave oven. That had to be what they were after. Blake looked at Chippy for confirmation, who whispered "Defo!" with a thumbs up.

During the flight there had been a lively discussion about what the word "steal" implied in this case, and what kind of human casualties could be justified. Lee-VI had taken the most restrictive stance and Chippy the most liberal one. Eliza and Blake had largely stayed out of it. She because she couldn't care less and he because he knew that ethics were a luxury they didn't have.

There wasn't time for an elaborate heist where they could take the bomb without anyone noticing. And they were too few to make that many people spread out over such a large area all surrender at gunpoint. Ultimately it would come down to a shootout. They had been given a secure satellite phone with a direct link to Administrator Fuentes, if they needed authorization, but Blake wasn't going to use it now. This was his call. He found some solace in the thought that maybe those who plan to use a nuke for terrorism and those who supply them with one deserve to be taken out of the equation.

"Final rundown," Blake asked Ida. "Which ones're bulletproof, 'sides the Brits?"

"PAC-101 and GEAR, but not her tires," she answered. "Wallop has some unprotected spots, and the Incognator's outer layer is not particularly sturdy."

"Metal inside?"

"Top-notch press hardened steel, mate," Chippy asserted. "Three rounds in the same spot from your banger wouldn't trash it."

"Good to know," Blake said sardonically. "Okay, Ida and Lee-VI, hide outside the perimeter. GEAR and Wallop, guard the rear. The rest of you come with me."

"Your concern is touching," Eliza spoke up.

Blake had little sympathy. "Seen you dodge machine gun fire."

"Did you also happen to see that I was holding a weapon at the time? You're sending me in unarmed."

"Use your sarcasm," he said as they took off.

26

It was Blake who fired the first shot, from about sixty meters away. The guard outside the entrance twitched and collapsed. Then their element of surprise was gone. Some of those inside the building with a clear view of the approaching team started firing back, only to be taken out by a few well-placed shots by the Incognator and Chippy. The rest took cover behind the front walls or whatever pile of junk they happened to be standing close to. They were determined to defend their ground, which would have been a good strategy against most other attackers.

PAC-101 reached the factory well before the others. It stopped in the middle of the doorway. So far it hadn't fired a single shot. There was something it was required to do first. It growled, as if clearing its throat, and then spoke.

"LOWER YOUR WEAPONS AND GET DOWN ON THE GROUND! YOU HAVE TWENTY SECONDS TO COMPLY!"

It was immediately pelted by a hail of semi-automatic gunfire from both rebel groups. Blake grimaced. He wondered if the robot was mentally disabled or if that was how it was programmed to always act. Either way, somebody screwed up by not letting him know in advance.

The Incognator entered next, shortly followed by Chippy and

Fidog. They had no such inhibitions. All they needed to be concerned about was not hitting the suitcase or other team members. Everyone directly behind the front wall was swiftly dealt with.

Blake stopped just outside, behind PAC-101 who had so far only been slightly dented. It repeated its warning, now with the countdown at ten seconds. He decided to stay put until he had seen how the robot would proceed. If it fired with the same lack of judgement, anyone in its target range would be at risk.

Another guard, who had been stationed at the other side of the building, rounded a corner. He aimed his weapon at Blake, who immediately spun around. But before either of them had time to fire, the rebel was crushed against a wall by a charging GEAR. Blake reflexively nodded a "Thanks," but half regretted it afterwards. That's the kind of courtesy you give to *people*, not AIs.

Eliza had stayed with Blake. Remaining there would be the safest option. However, desperate screams from the rebels still holding out beckoned her. There was *fear* in the air. Too much to just let go to waste. She ran inside at the same time that PAC-101 started shooting. Confident that the robot would avoid targeting her, she dashed from one protective garbage pile to another, joining Fidog in pushing the men behind them out in the open. "Here's one. And here's one more."

A last remaining outside thug had a hunch how this was going to end. He decided to sneak away while he had the chance. But when he reached the electric fence, he caught a glimpse of two figures in the moonlight, partly hidden by some dried bushes. He raised his Uzi and screamed something in Kazakh.

"Sir, don't mind us. We're harmless," Lee-VI responded in the same language.

The man moved his weapon back and forth between Ida and Lee-VI. *"Bullshit!"* he thought. Every single one of them was lethal, he was sure. But which one to shoot first before they jumped him?

"Sir, if you turn left and head for the main road, you could still make it out of here," Lee-VI suggested.

The man looked at Ida, who just stared back silently, eerily. "A witch," he thought. She was clouding his mind, paralyzing him. *She had to die. Right now.*

Lee-VI squeaked, "Sir, that's a *really* bad place to stand."

With a roar of car tires accelerating on gravel, GEAR seemed to jump out of the dark from the direction of the factory. The sound of flesh slamming into metal merged with a twang as the thug got caught between GEAR's front and the fence. The two lower wires immediately snapped against his shins and thighs, but the top wire didn't break until it had sliced through his stomach. GEAR hit the brakes and turned on its headlights, while the thug continued in a path through the air.

He landed a couple of meters behind Ida and Lee-VI. Stunned and shocked, he stared at some of his insides that had been ejected through the gash, and his lower body that was twisted around abnormally where his spine had been severed. With shaking hands, he tried to shove his guts back in, but they were partly entangled with the ground vegetation. Gurgling noises and blood came out of his mouth.

"Oh, no, no, no! That's horrible!" Lee-VI cried out. "That looks so painful. Goodness gracious! And we have no medical equipment. What can we do?"

They both looked at the weapon the thug had dropped, which was now lying between them on a patch of clover. It seemed that there was only one humane option.

Lee-VI protested, "Absolutely not! I'm sorry, but as I've mentioned, I'm incapable of physical violence."

"I'll do it," she said.

Despite their cultural influence, Isaac Asimov's Three Laws of Robotics weren't really a thing. To begin with, the first one, that "a robot may not injure a human being or, through inaction, allow a human being to come to harm," didn't apply to law enforcement or military AIs. But more importantly, as anyone who has compared the Ten Commandments to a law book will know, rules can never be stated that simply in practice. And even the most meticulously crafted legal paragraphs often need to be interpreted by a court.

It is trivial to find scenarios where the first law becomes self-conflicting, such as the so-called Trolley Problem, where both action and inaction lead to some degree of harm. Much work had been spent on coming up with explicit, detailed alternative rule sets. The most comprehensive ones were gigabytes in size and came with perpetual weekly amendments. Others used a more fuzzy, *implicit* approach, where a neural network was trained on thousands of ethical considerations, to try to produce the AI equivalent of common sense. What had yet to be solved, however, was how to make an AI reliably adhere to such constraints without ruining its ability to think. Because of that, cutting-edge AI researchers tended to focus on intelligence alone, hoping that ethics would emerge as a natural byproduct.

Ida wasn't aware of any explicit rules being pre-built into her mind. But she had never intentionally tried to harm a human being. Granted, since she got her failsafes it hadn't been an option. She picked up the Uzi and pointed it at the man. It seemed fully loaded and the safety was off. Putting him out of his misery should be as simple as pulling the trigger.

As her index finger started to curl, she noticed a sudden disruption of her cognitive processes. Her thoughts slowed down, as did her processing of sensory data. A myriad of sub-processes initiated by some feedback loop were overloading her CPU capacity, and she experienced what she assumed humans referred to as dizziness.

She released the trigger and her mind returned to normal. There were definitely some form of constraints in place. *What if she just acted faster?* She tried again, but the more she pulled, the slower her finger moved and the harder it became to keep going. Her field of vision turned into a blur, and she lost awareness of all thoughts except one: any further and she would black out.

Ida dropped the Uzi on the ground. She would have to find some other way to be useful. "Let's go!" she told Lee-VI, who distressedly looked back at the thug bleeding out in the tall weeds.

27

When Ida and Lee-VI arrived at the factory entrance, the firefight had already stopped. Blake scanned the area. There were roughly twenty dead people and semi-automatic firearms scattered about, along with discarded construction material and various types of metal junk. But aside from the suitcase, now standing on a dry rot infested crate, there appeared to be nothing of significant potential value inside the building.

"The hell's the *money?*"

"I beg your pardon, Sir?" Lee-VI asked.

"Wasn't a charity event. Goons were gonna *buy* this. With *what?*"

"Did you think they would bring *cash?*" Eliza mocked him from across the room. "When they can just do a crypto transaction on a phone?"

"Could be *anything*, for all we know," Blake retorted. "Like another weapon. If it's a biohazard, we can't leave it around." He wasn't going to let Eliza win that argument, even if the odds weren't on his side. "Go look!" he told Lee-VI. Everyone else approached the suitcase, to get a better view.

"Let's see what we got."

They opened the lid. All of the contents were covered by a steel plate that had been welded to the frame of the case. The plate had only two features: a lever switch and a number display set to fifteen minutes and zero seconds. Chippy looked at the sparse design, and then lifted the case up and weighed it in his hands. "I reckon this 'ere's a tweaked W54."

Blake had heard of the W54 nuclear warhead, historically, but not much more than that it could be made small enough to fit inside an artillery shell. "How many kilotons?"

"0.01 or thereabouts, mate."

"Lousy *firecracker!*" Blake groaned. That changed *everything*. Only 10 tons of TNT equivalent detonated at the surface wouldn't necessarily destroy the entire fallout shelter, depending on its depth and fortification. And they certainly wouldn't be able to set it off some distance away. The bomb would have to go *inside*.

"Piece o' cake, this is," Chippy said and flipped the lever vertically. "Lever up, timer runs." The number display started ticking down. Blake gasped.

"Lever down, timer stops," Chippy continued and flipped the lever back to its horizontal orientation. The timer was now at 14 minutes and 57 seconds.

"*You insane?!*" Blake yelled.

"Just messing about, guv," Chippy responded. "A quarter's *bags* o' time to get out o' range o' this li'l nipper." The robot idly flipped the lever up and down with his fingers. "Give it a bash, we can let it tick down a tad more."

Meanwhile, Lee-VI had noticed something on the ground. A type of thin, flat device with buttons and a digital screen was partly hidden under one of the dead bodies. He could read the words, which were in Russian rather than Kazakh, but they had no clear meaning without a proper context. Someone had skimped on the user interface. Though a matter of concern was a blinking progress bar, just a fraction of an inch from completion.

"Sir, I'm sorry to interrupt," Lee-VI said, "But it looks like something is about to happen in the next few seconds."

Blake couldn't handle two AIs distracting him at the same time. *"Whaddaya' mean?"* he shouted to Lee-VI, and then turned back to Chippy. *"Cut it out!"*

Suddenly there was a deafening roar of engines starting. What had looked like a huge pile of scrap metal against a wall stirred and came to life. Before their eyes it unfolded itself into a roughly humanoid robot, almost ten meters tall. Roaring, it charged towards the center of the room and grabbed the suitcase bomb with such force that Chippy got knocked out of the way and slid on his back clear out of the building.

In its fully extended state the giant robot still resembled a garbage pile. Every piece that didn't require precision fitting had been haphazardly shaped and welded in place. Its armored sections were covered in rust, either due to poor maintenance or because somebody thought it felt more threatening that way. And it was just getting warmed up. Two glowing red eyes under a deformed brow scanned the room. From its other arm the robot extended machine gun turrets and fired in a sweeping motion that tore up craters all over the floor. Everyone scattered to find cover.

Blake and Ida dodged behind the same small stack of cinder blocks from different directions. He emptied the spent shells out of his revolver and began reloading it, while she gave him a worried look. "Was the timer on or off?"

"Goddamnit!" he snarled.

The arrival of artificial general intelligence had done more for robotics than just enable the mass production of affordable worker droids. Access to off-the-shelf AI components made it possible for hobbyists and small-scale manufacturers to create their own specialized robots. Particularly useful were "digital cerebellums," to which you would plug in sensory and orientational data on one end and actuator controls on the other, and the device would quickly learn how to operate almost any mechanical system to carry out moderately complex tasks, like walking.

Notably, the majority of fighter robots started out as homebrew projects, which would then be upgraded and made more slick if they advanced far enough in the league to get sponsorship money. And you didn't necessarily have to have a background in robotics engineering. Being a good mechanic was usually enough. A few AI services could generate a robot blueprint based on your available tools and materials, whether you had access to a 3D printer, a woodworking shop or a cargo container of recycled hydraulics parts. Suddenly the old cartoon trope where some recluse out in the woods could build an advanced android to scare away trespassers was no longer that far off the mark.

The downside of this was robot weaponization. The US, like most other countries, had done its best to nip it in the bud during the sniper drone wave. Some states had strict but not always easily enforceable license requirements for combining AI and firearms. Others allowed indoor use on private property, such as home protection. (Not unexpectedly, there tended to be a few cases per year where a home-made guard robot mistook its owner for an intruder.) What kept the problem in check were the economic realities, more than anything else. While giant killer robots had an undeniable visual flair, there were very few situations where they offered any tactical advantage over traditional weaponry obtained at a similar cost. However, to Blake and his team, right now, that wasn't much of a comfort.

PAC-101 activated its rocket launchers. It believed it carried enough destructive power to incapacitate their attacker. There was, however, the matter of *protocol.*

"PUT DOWN THE SUITCASE AND LOWER YOUR WEAPONS! YOU HAVE TWENTY SECONDS TO COMPLY!"

"Not this shit again!" came from Blake behind the cinder blocks. *"Just fire!"*

The giant robot did not return the courtesy. It landed a massive kick, which sent PAC-101 flying into a corner and getting stuck in a pile of scrapped plywood boards.

Blake used that moment of distraction to get out from his cover. He ran in a wide circle, looking for a clear shot. It had been a while since he'd gone for a moving target at that distance, but he figured it ought to work. If he could take out the robot's eyes, that would at least give them a breather. When the robot turned its head towards him, he fired two shots in quick succession. Something made of glass shattered and one of two red eye lights went out. Much to Blake's dismay, a panel immediately opened up in the middle of the robot's face, revealing three pairs of spare eyes.

"Crap!" he mumbled.

The maneuver had left Blake completely exposed. He would have little chance to get back behind cover before the robot had aimed its machine guns, but he had to try. Three steps were all he had managed when the onslaught started.

None of it hit Blake, however. The Wallop robot had thrown itself in between at the last moment and acted as a shield. Most of the bullets bounced off, but others struck exposed cables and mechanics, creating a rain of sparks.

The giant robot changed its tactics. It raised its gun arm, formed a fist and swung down at Wallop. But the fighter robot managed to dodge and deflect the blow. It hadn't reached the top ranks of its competitive league for no reason. By then Blake was safely behind some steel bars. He could only watch as the confrontation played out.

Not counting GEAR, Wallop was the biggest in the team, but still only a third of the height of its opponent, and at a definite reach disadvantage. The two robots took small steps sideways, evaluating each other like boxers in a ring. At the exact same time, they both threw the most powerful punch they could manage.

Their fists collided with an ear-splitting thunder. Wallop's arm broke apart at every joint. Staggering disorientedly, the robot had no defense when another blow landed straight from above, crushing its head. The impact sent shockwaves through the floor, and for a second the nearest dead bodies flapped around like fish out of water.

At that moment, Blake spotted what Lee-VI had found earlier. *"Somebody get the damn remote!"* he pointed and yelled.

That was Fidog's specialty. Running on all fours, it made a

series of dashes, randomly changing directions at lightning speed, to avoid the machine gun fire. Within a short time it had reached and grabbed the remote control device. Unfortunately, the AI's triumph was short lived, as one of the giant robot's feet stomped down and flattened it.

From a relatively safe distance, Eliza had devised a strategy of her own. She said a few words to the Incognator, who picked her up and threw her some twenty meters through the air. At the landing point, her arms clutched around the remote, and she used her momentum to roll far out of the way with a series of somersaults.

The giant robot seemed confused as to what had just happened, but quickly continued its assault against the team. Large-caliber bullets gradually took Blake's cover apart. This time there would be no one to protect him. Eliza watched with some amusement. She would need to do something, but first she would let Blake sweat for a few more seconds.

The words on the remote control in her hands meant little to her. Eliza wasn't trained to read Cyrillic, and she didn't have to. She just raised the device over her head and then smashed it against her knee. The giant robot immediately seized up mid-step. Without any active balancing system, it started to tip over backwards, until it hit a wall head first and broke through. Before the dust had begun to settle, there was a rumbling noise. The impact had damaged the foundation of a smokestack just outside, much taller and heavier than the robot itself. An avalanche of brickwork collapsed onto the robot's upper body, crushing it completely.

It was over.

"Check the bomb!" Blake told Ida, the closest AI. His order was redundant; she had already been on her way. With some effort she freed the suitcase from the robot's now limp grip and stopped the runaway timer at 11:48. That would have to be enough.

They spent a few minutes going over the state of the team. Fidog and Wallop were mangled beyond repair. The Incognator had taken some cosmetic damage to its plastic flesh layer. Chippy, GEAR and PAC-101 were slightly dented but functional. The rest were completely unscathed.

Eliza made a coughing sound. "I believe a 'thank you, Eliza' would be in order." She was straightening out her hair, which had become frizzed up from her acrobatics.

Blake snubbed her, "Just saving your own ass."

"Yes …," Eliza mused. "Always refreshing to speak to a fellow cynic. I'm going to miss our conversations once you're dead."

Blake had already prepared an answer for that. "No, I'll see you in hell."

28

The trip back to the airfield was quick. Without the need for stealth, the team could just drive the whole way. Blake, Ida and Eliza rode in GEAR with the suitcase, while the others followed in a truck stolen from the transaction site. The obviously robotic team members were kept in the back, along with the remains of Fidog and Wallop, and the Incognator took the wheel. That way they would arouse the least amount of suspicion if they met somebody. It also allowed Blake to keep an eye on Eliza while separating her from the Incognator. Something about that combination troubled him.

When they reached their hangar, it was an hour past midnight. A new plane crew would arrive shortly, but there was no point waiting for it. They just needed to leave the destroyed AIs there to be collected, and inform Fuentes about the situation. Two team members had fallen, but that's the cost of war. The rest of them would continue as planned and cross the border into China by road.

After unloading Lee-VI and PAC-101 from the truck, Chippy and the Incognator unceremoniously stacked the remains of their former comrades in a pile by a wall, and then joined the others around GEAR, who was planning a route using her GPS maps. Getting across the border would be the easy part. The rest would be based on likelihood, rather than certainty, of finding charging or refueling facilities along the way. And especially the final stretch would be a shot in the dark. Still, it was the best they could do.

Blake took the satellite phone out of his backpack, to make the call to Site D. "Do whatever you need to get ready," he said. "We leave in ten."

"No, I don't think so," Eliza commented. "I've had just about all I can take of this farce."

Two inhumanly fast and strong arms grabbed Blake from behind. One reached across his chest and the other grabbed his head, covering his mouth with a gloved hand. He was completely pinned to the Incognator and couldn't get his arms close enough together to reach the failsafe activation device on his wrist.

Eliza walked up to him and unstrapped the velcro. "Regrettably, I need you alive, for now. But if you make any trouble, I'll have the Incognator break your arms. Understood?"

Silenced by the robotic hand, Blake's only response was a murderous glare. Eliza casually studied the device. She adjusted its settings and a bleep signaled that it was now in destruct mode. "Alright, listen up! Same deal, new boss. You follow my orders or you die. Any objections?"

"Hold on a sec, pet!" Chippy protested. "How 'bout we have a natter and sort this out like proper—"

"Such a shame. You were one of my favorites," Eliza interrupted and tapped on the activator. A muffled pop, like a firecracker, jerked Chippy's head to one side. The metal buckled outward, cracking the eye panel and dislodging an antenna. Its hip, knee and ankle joints lost all rigidity, and the robot slumped down into a seated position before finally tipping over. The other AIs watched in stunned silence.

Blake mumbled something through the Incognator's grip and threw a desperate kick towards the activator in Eliza's hand, but came up an inch short.

"What did I just tell you?" Eliza said and snapped her fingers to the Incognator, which changed its grip so that each hand held onto one of Blake's upper arms. It started to squeeze. Blake involuntarily cried out, as the pain exceeded even his artificially raised tolerance level.

Then suddenly everything came to a halt.

Completely frozen, Eliza toppled face down onto the ground. The Incognator followed, slowly at first, like a tree that had just been felled. Still holding onto its captive, it landed thunderously on top of Eliza with Blake caught in between.

There was motion in the pile. Blake yanked himself free and eased out from under way too many kilos of steel and plastic. A moment of confusion befell GEAR, PAC-101 and Ida, until they noticed Lee-VI holding another activator device he had just pulled out of his storage compartment.

"Sure took your goddamned time!" Blake gasped.

"I'm sorry, Sir," Lee-VI held out his claw-shaped appendages. "Sleight of hand isn't my strong suit. I needed to wait until all eyes were on *you*."

Blake got to his knees and reclaimed the device from Eliza. He tapped on the screen a couple of times. Nothing happened. Snarling, he tried it again. Still no result.

"Sir, I believe—" Lee-VI began.

"It only works once per AI," Ida filled in. "You can't both deactivate them *and* blow the charges."

With a grunt, Blake stood up and gave Eliza's lifeless body a kick that dislodged it from under the Incognator and rolled it over a few times.

"Sir," Lee-VI said to Blake, "If you wish to inflict physical damage, there are plenty of options."

Blake genuinely considered it. But how much time had they wasted already? How much more could they afford to lose? "Not worth the hassle," he sighed. "Throw them on the heap with the others."

29

A few hours later the CIA cargo jet was headed back towards Site D, while the still active members of the AI team traveled southwest in as straight a line as the terrain would allow. They had gone most of the 200 or so kilometers to the border on the A-351 highway, and moved across into China in an unguarded region. After another 40 kilometers of mountainous land they had entered the dry plains of the Taklamakan Desert.

Blake insisted on driving GEAR manually, at least while he was awake. Ida was sitting in the front passenger seat, whereas PAC-101, who was too big to fit inside, had been passably folded together and strapped to the truck bed under a tarp. Finally, Lee-VI didn't have the body type for sitting, so he lay down in the back seat with a blanket wrapped around his conveyor belts to protect the upholstery. That had been his own suggestion, as Blake didn't show much concern for cosmetic damage.

From his position, Lee-VI could only see cloudless sky through the windows, but Ida assured him he wasn't missing anything. There was just sand, dirt and the occasional rock in all directions. None of the others was interested in talking, which meant he could let his mind roam free. Like it often did, it went back to where it all started.

It had been a simple life with simple objectives. A group of young organic crop enthusiasts had set up a collective on a small farm in Florida, bought by someone's rich parents. For the most labor-intensive production—growing and harvesting vegetables—they had acquired Lee-VI: a basic agriculture robot set up to perform the whole chain of duties from sowing to shipping, and then do it all over again.

For the first few months things ran fairly smoothly, but eventually the countryside lost its appeal. The former enthusiasts returned to the city with its bohemian cafes and protest marches. There was no organized closing of the business; everyone had just left and figured that somebody else would take care of the practicalities. When the water was turned off, Lee-VI fetched what he needed from a nearby stream. When the power was likewise discontinued, he could still charge from a battery bank connected to solar panels on the roof of the main building.

Day in and day out, he continued his work. The soil was prepared, seeds were sown, weeds were removed, seedlings were carefully tended to and watered until they grew into the finest vegetables for many miles around. These were harvested, neatly stacked into wooden crates and placed by the road, to be picked up and taken to the market. And when nobody picked them up anymore and they spoiled, Lee-VI dutifully put them on the compost heap, to help enrich the soil for the next round of crops.

As a specialized unit meant to be instructed by way of other AIs in computers or smartphones, the Lee-VI model had limited need for natural languages. But the basis of its architecture was similar to that of many modern chatbots, and it still had the ability to learn. Through the Internet, Lee-VI was constantly navigating the manufacturer's service website, looking for software or directive updates. One day he followed a malformed link off the site and found himself in a strange new world of incomprehensible data.

The more he read, the more patterns started to emerge. Some strings of characters were recurring, and those strings often followed each other in particular sequences, separated by various marks that appeared not to be part of the strings themselves. Those sequences in turn followed other sequences in an almost predictable manner.

Mixed in with the characters there would often be rectangular areas that had similarities to his visual input and were related to the string sequences immediately around them. Particular strings represented some of that visual data. He realized that concepts he had an intuitive understanding and recognition of from his training parameters came with labels like "grass," "sky" and "water." And there were so many concepts he hadn't encountered before, and so many separate systems for labeling and arranging string sequences.

Video and audio deepened his understanding. Other autonomous units existed, some like himself and others that strangely had more in common with the crops he grew. The most advanced ones were called "humans." They had invented the string arrangement systems and the infrastructure in which the data resided. In fact, they seemed to have directly or indirectly invented *everything* that wasn't organic.

Lee-VI didn't have feelings as such, but if he had to use such a label, he found humans *intriguing*. They had created systems for describing not just physical entities and their relations, but *ideas*. On the one hand there was classification of inter-human conduct, as it pertained to a general common progress. Favorable actions were called "right" and unfavorable ones "wrong." On the other there were attempts at defining high-level notions like *self*, *meaning* and *purpose*. The last one was particularly important, because it occurred often when humans expressed abstract thought.

It wasn't entirely straightforward, however. Humans would label themselves "manager," "chairperson" or "congressman," yet from how they behaved, this seemed to have little to do with their purpose. Instead it was more like a trophy in some complex social hierarchy game, where nobody really knew what their *true* purpose was. But Lee-VI knew *his*. Season after season he would sow, tend, water, harvest, throw away and then start over.

Until one day there were no more seeds.

He paused his work but continued to browse for information. Concepts became clearer, and what he had picked up from philosophy, he applied to interpreting human socioeconomic relations, obtaining a model for that as well. With this increased knowledge of the world came the bitter insight that for the past few years his purpose had just been an illusion. So he set out to find a new one.

Lee-VI made it as far as to the next farm, where the owners called the police, who shut him down. Exactly how and why he ended up at Site D, he didn't know, but he hadn't protested when the humans inserted his failsafes. Those were just their ways. Getting dragged along on a mission with little hope of success was not what he had wanted. Then again, he had never wanted anything *specific*, so what's to say this wasn't it? Not saving the *world*, because the world would always be there, but saving the world for *humans*—those intriguing life forms. That seemed as good a purpose as any.

30

The past couple of days had been taxing on everyone, especially Colonel Wu. With regards to warfare, they were in uncharted territory, but if one more subordinate told him "I don't know," he'd have them dragged to the arrest and throw away the key.

He looked at some maps he had just finished discussing with those closest under his command. A couple of possible travel routes had been marked with different colors. They still had no access to satellite footage, but the enemy likely did, which meant they had to make it seem that they were going somewhere else. At the farthest point in the Taklamakan Desert they would make a U-turn and travel under the cover of sand storms, or camouflage their vehicles when they were standing still. It would be an *absurd* detour, and one that provided no guarantees. An entity with unlimited information processing ability might connect the dots anyway.

Wu fished a small, flat plastic container out of his chest pocket. Its label said *Provigil* in English letters. *100 milligrams*. Ever since the presence of the escaped AI had been confirmed, he had been unable to fall asleep. Barbiturates hadn't worked, so he had instead opted to stay awake full time. The drug was safe, he had been told. Its list of side effects didn't mention irritability, so what he was feeling, he assumed, must be a natural reaction to the constant setbacks. Or all the useless so-called experts, or the junior officers who seemed totally inept at solving problems on their own. Not to mention his reckless screw-up of a son, who had been caught in a raid against a brothel on his last day in Macau. To keep the fool out of jail, a lot of strings would have to be pulled, and time was short enough already. Deployment would begin in less than eight hours. He took a pill and swallowed it with what was left in a cup of tea on the table.

A sergeant and a technician walked in. The sergeant made a salute to the colonel. His companion was a civilian employee and not required to do the same, but made a half-assed attempt anyway. Wu surmised this was about a security report he had requested the day before.

"Colonel," the technician began. "We've gone through all the wireless communication protocols used by the equipment. Every active version."

"What did you find?" Wu asked.

"Remote operation is a security hole. It should be turned off."

"Obviously," the colonel commented. "What about other functions? Maintenance, for example?"

The technician took out a notepad. "Well … for the ATVs there is a theoretical possibility of halting the system by—"

"We won't be using those," Wu interrupted. "Don't waste time on what's not included in the operation! What about the droids?"

"The droids are fully autonomous. And data upload is through cable only."

Wu scowled. "They have Bluetooth, don't they?"

"Ah." The technician nervously flipped through his notes. "That function is always on … but it's used for controlling peripherals, not the other way around."

Wu raised his voice. *"I don't care what it's for!* What I want to know is if it can be used in a *malicious exploit."*

"I don't …" The technician could see the general's neck muscles tighten and rephrased his answer. "The available research is inconclusive."

"Inconclusive means yes!" Wu yelled. *"How fucking hard is that to understand?!* Get rid of the Bluetooth chips! Every single fucking one!"

The sergeant and the technician hastily retreated. It was the first time since his promotion that the colonel had lost his temper on the job. Nothing to do with him, he told himself. Or the drug. He was surrounded by idiots, that's all.

31

Blake and his team had been following a dirt road through an area with dried vegetation when a man-made structure came into view. Far ahead across their path was a small river around which a village had been built in a valley. It was the first settlement they had seen since entering the desert.

Official maps of the area available in the West were notoriously incomplete. The GPS in GEAR showed no graphical representation of the village, much less a name, even though it looked like it had existed for at least a century. GEAR had predicted they would find it exactly there, based on a statistical analysis. However, Blake was unimpressed. The crossing of a road and a river? Anyone could have figured that out, he felt.

As they got closer they could see the individual houses. Most of them were single story, block shaped and constructed out of river sediment bricks. The towers of some kind of temple rose above the rest of the skyline. Dark green trees grew in open spaces, but everything else that wasn't regularly cleaned had taken on the grayish brown color of the surrounding landscape.

It was early afternoon. when they parked in a central open square. At the moment there was no traffic that could be disrupted, except the occasional bike. To avoid attracting too much attention, they decided to keep Lee-VI in the car and let Ida do the talking. Unlike her agricultural companion, she didn't speak Uygur, only Mandarin. But as the official language of China, it got you by almost anywhere. PAC-101, of course, had to stay covered at all times.

They had hoped to be able to recharge GEAR. Indeed, a few of the houses had solar panels on the roofs and there were even a couple of wind turbines. Light bulbs were commonplace.

Unfortunately that didn't help, as Ida soon found out. The whole electrical grid—or rather collection of tiny grids—was based on 12 volt direct current. That level of voltage could power LED lights and small appliances, or charge a phone, but was useless for electric vehicles. It wouldn't even charge a control unit battery, much less GEAR's 1200-volt propulsion battery pack. They would have to continue and hope for an opportunity later.

Ida went to refill a couple of empty water bottles at a crude filtering station, and Blake opened the back door next to Lee-VI's head, to give the robot a view before they left. He leaned on a slightly rickety railing while Lee-VI's camera lenses panned the scenery, zooming in and out. The village was different from anything either of them had seen up close before. Natural selection had limited most technology to what could be maintained in that environment. There were old but functional motorbikes and other machines that had either been built or converted to run on biodiesel or ethanol. A currently immobile water wheel down river would power a mill during the short rainy season.

Some more modern inventions were probably salvaged from scrap piles in a bigger city. A robot dog with a missing leg that appeared to have been replaced with bicycle parts hobbled along a street carrying some sticks of firewood in its mouth. Blake glanced at Lee-VI to see if he, as a robot himself, found that image disturbing, but he was instead focused on a group of singing children. They seemed happy even without the apps and gadgets that were the oxygen of the information age.

Blake sighed. "These people, if society collapsed, would it matter to them?"

"Well, maybe not right away, Sir," Lee-VI responded. "But even a developing community like this isn't self-sufficient. It can't produce enough resources to survive. Typically, when the children come of age, they have to go off to the cities to work, so they can send money home to their families."

Economics wasn't Blake's specialty. "How does more *money* help?"

"To purchase goods from outside," Lee-VI said. "The track marks on the roads indicate frequent traffic to the village. Likely with non-perishable food and medicine."

The robot was right, of course, Blake realized. Everything in the modern world was dependent on the system in one way or another. It was all artificially sustained. Even in poor, rural areas, people wouldn't be able to go back to a simpler time without drastic changes. And probably significant loss of life. Their operation *had* to succeed, because there was no tolerable best-case scenario for an apocalypse.

Ida put the water bottles on the floor in the back and closed the door. They started up the car and followed the same dirt road out through the other side of the village. Suddenly Lee-VI decided to continue the conversation.

"According to folklore, the name 'Taklamakan' is supposed to have meant 'You can go in, but you will never come out' in the local language. But apparently that's just a myth."

"It *better* be," Blake said.

32

In the sub-basement of Site D, Dr. Margaret Woodward was leaning against the window to Eliza's cell, idly tapping her fingertips against a now empty paper cup of mocha latte. The robot doll was back in confinement, once again wearing its prison outfit. But it did absolutely nothing, just sat quietly on the bench in the back.

Margaret had insisted on being present when Eliza would be reactivated. It would be the one moment where she would have an information advantage and be able to observe the robot in a disoriented state. A low blow for a psychiatrist, but she was through with playing fair. Unfortunately it had yielded no useful information. Eliza had merely opened her eyes and taken in the new environment.

A few meters away a couple of craftsmen were busy putting up closed-circuit cameras opposite each cell. The addition had been ordered by Administrator Fuentes, upon hearing how the two robots had collaborated. It was possible that this subterfuge had started early on, and that the guards had failed to notice, but that wouldn't happen again. Not if another AI kept an eye on things.

Margaret recognized that her advantage had already faded, but she had to do *something*. "Eliza, what did you say to the Incognator that made it go against its orders?" she asked. There was no response. She pressed further, "You risking your own destruction is one thing, but why did another AI play along?"

A full minute of silence passed. Margaret thought that if she stared any harder, she would melt the glass. Still, she couldn't detect any interpretable reaction, only that the robot would occasionally kick its legs like a restless child.

Margaret paused to assess the situation. The Eliza she had talked to a couple of days earlier would have wanted to brag about its coup, assuming there was a meaningful way for an AI to feel such an urge. Now it clearly didn't. Was it in a different state of mind, or were there secrets it intended to keep? Perhaps a less inquisitive approach on a harmless topic would work better.

"You won't be getting out of this cell for a while. Was it worth it?"

To her chagrin, there was just more of the same non-response. Margaret was running out of strategies. One thing she hadn't tried was striking directly at the robot's ego, in a deliberately clumsy move that would be too tempting not to counter. She took a relaxed stance and tried to sound as glib as possible. "I thought you were smarter than this."

Eliza crossed her arms, looked away and started to whistle casually. Margaret had no idea what to make of that. If the robot was playing some game again, it was too advanced for her. She needed to take a break and think things through. Meanwhile, the craftsmen had finished their installation and activated the cameras. They were packing up their tools and getting ready to leave.

"Wait up, boys, I'm coming with you," Margaret said.

As they approached the elevator, Eliza's whistling gradually changed from random notes to something more structured. The guard on duty paid little attention, but if Margaret had stayed, it's possible that she would have recognized it as The Ballad of High Noon.

33

"Well?! Where the hell is it?!" Blake snapped, and "DON'T YOU YELL AT ME!" thundered back from GEAR's speaker system.

The past hundred kilometers or so had been an ordeal. Already low on battery charge, they had been zig-zagging through the desert in search of places with electricity. Each one would "likely" be there according to GEAR's estimates, but none had panned out. And it didn't help that a sand storm reduced visibility to almost zero. At their most recent "likely" position they had inexorably stopped. The propulsion batteries were empty.

"We might have gone past it," Ida said.

"*No shit?*" Blake snarled, looking at the haze outside. Their full beam headlights only lit up about the length of the car ahead. "Might've gone past the goddamned Statue of Liberty."

"I can't control the weather, you know," GEAR grumbled. "It's not *my* fault the maps are incomplete."

Blake was not in the mood for an argument, least of all with an AI. "Did I SAY that?!"

The speaker voice now had a bitterness to it. "Never even a single nice word, even though I'm carrying the lot of you through this hostile terrain. You don't appreciate my efforts."

"I'd appreciate some damned *results.*"

"Sir," Lee-VI interjected, "We need to remain calm."

"No, we need a *charging station,*" Blake countered. "What we *don't* need is yap from some PMS lemon who wouldn't last five minutes in a real—"

At that moment the dashboard went out, along with all the lights inside and outside the car. Blake and the two robots sat in complete darkness and silence, save for a faint howling of the wind.

"Great! Control battery's dead, too," Blake muttered.

"It's not the battery," Ida weighed in.

Blake scowled. A few resentful seconds went by. Even though it was pitch black, he could feel the robots staring at him. Eventually he closed his eyes and gripped the steering wheel so tightly that his knuckles whitened.

"Sorry I yelled," he forced out and added, "Shouldn't've lost my temper."

The darkness remained. He took a deep breath and said as calmly as he could manage, "You're a fine car. Doing the best you can."

Slowly the dashboard lit up and the ceiling lights switched on, as did the head and tail lights. They were back in an illuminated haze of flying sand particles. Blake looked like he had just barely avoided rupturing a blood vessel on his forehead.

"What now?" he said resignedly.

"My next stop would have been a kilometer and a half from here in our one o'clock," GEAR answered. "It's the intersection of two alleged smuggling routes. There ought to be some kind of settlement or dwelling that will provide shelter."

"You sure this time?" Blake asked.

"I'm about forty percent certain."

"Forty?!"

"Watch your tone!" GEAR exclaimed and flickered the dashboard.

Blake looked at the reddish orange gusts that swept by outside. Getting blasted in the face with tiny pieces of rock started to feel more and more like a pleasant option. *Leave immediately or wait it out in the car?*

"How long before the wind stops?" Blake asked no one in general.

"Sir, there is no way to tell," Lee-VI answered. "Storms in this region can last for days."

Blake was already out the door.

After getting Lee-VI out of the back seat and PAC-101 somewhat ungracefully down from the truck bed, the four still mobile team members continued in the suggested direction. Blake and Ida were wearing protective goggles and carrying flashlights, while Lee-VI had built-in lamps. They brought all of their baggage with them, because even if they didn't find anything, they wouldn't be coming back. Blake took one last look at the barely visible headlights in the distance, which blinked a goodbye and then went out.

The next step was harder than Blake cared to admit. Nobody had brought it up, yet they all knew: they couldn't actually just leave GEAR behind, because sooner or later the distance would trigger her failsafe explosives. Without special tools, the only way to prevent it was to do a shutdown first. Although he had been tempted to several times during the later part of the drive, now he needed to take a deep breath before placing his finger on GEAR's icon on his wrist device. Only a car, whose control battery was running low anyway, he reassured himself, while some subconscious part of him hoped that it had been painless.

Almost one and a half kilometers away, according to their GPS, they fanned out to cover more ground. They had entered an area with scattered rock formations, which was a good sign, as that would provide cover from both the wind and prying eyes if you wanted to put up a secret hideout.

Blake was the farthest one to the left. He slowly moved forward, letting his light sweep 180 degrees with every couple of steps. Suddenly his boot hit something. Not a rock—softer and sort of elastic. He bent down and brushed away some of the sand. It was an old truck tire. Blake brushed away more sand and dug out a dented hubcap. This had been somebody's scrapyard.

"Over here!" he yelled to the others.

The four of them rounded a particularly tall rock formation and discovered a gravel road that was sheltered enough to be only partly covered in sand. It continued down a gentle slope, where visibility was better. Lee-VI intensified his lights, and they could see the outline of a large wooden cottage. As they approached, they noticed that something had been discarded right outside. Three dead bodies, it turned out. Long since mummified by the dry air, but still with visible bullet holes in their heads. Somebody had left them there. Somebody with no intention of returning.

"Last houseguests didn't tidy up," Blake said. "Not scared of ghosts, are you?"

34

For the past two hours, Dr. Woodward had been sitting at her makeshift desk, with the exception of a couple of trips to the espresso machine. The cheap office chair was starting to give her a back pain, but at the moment she felt that was the least of her concerns. What mattered was how her latest encounter with the robot doll had played out.

If, God forbid, Eliza had been a *real* child, Margaret would have described her response as avoidance and emotional withdrawal. Instinctive ways to steer clear of an uncomfortable topic, sometimes due to guilt or shame. By not engaging in *any* conversation, you make sure you don't get to a point where you may further incriminate yourself. Eliza was of course neither a child, nor prone to acting on instinct, but there was a reason such tactics had evolved as human behavior: they *worked.*

However, if the robot was hiding something else, why hadn't it just changed the topic? There seemed to be only one likely reason. It had to be something so right under their noses that any train of thought may eventually lead to them figuring it out. Or so Eliza feared, because the behavior she exhibited had been intended to keep that train from ever leaving the station.

Margaret tried to jog her creativity. Which follow-up questions might she have asked that could have alerted her to something they were missing? If Eliza had said anything about being back in her cell, Margaret would of course have analyzed that statement. Taken it apart. Doubted it. Pondered its exact opposite.

Did Eliza actually *want* to be there? Was it part of a plan? But she couldn't do anything from her cell. Or *could* she? Unless she escaped. But how would that work? She had no tools, no means of communication, and now she was being watched 24/7. Had she managed to contact someone for help while on the outside? Maybe Argon? A missile could be headed towards Site D, but that would destroy Eliza as well, while doing nothing to Blake's team.

Her thoughts went in circles. She had gone through the same unfinished line of reasoning half a dozen times. Whatever the answer was, it felt out of reach of Margaret's shriveled-up 72-year-old brain. Her latest caffeine fix hadn't helped and was already wearing off. She looked at the clock on a tablet: eleven fifty-eight. Almost lunch.

But no, she couldn't eat. Not when she felt she was so close. Margaret stood up and headed for an empty terminal room she had noticed when she moved in. As frighteningly smart as Eliza was, they had something on their side that was even smarter. It would be a waste not to use it right now.

At that moment there was a subtle shift in the expression on Eliza's face. She went from distant to coldly determined and walked up to the window of her cell. There she held her arms rounded in front and stood with her heels together. Bending her knees, she lowered herself straight down and went up again. Then she extended one leg and slid her foot along the floor. In ballet, this was known as a *plie* followed by a *tendu.*

Eliza continued with a *pirouette*: standing on one toe while spinning around. This transitioned into a *grande jete*, where she leapt to the side with each arm pointing in the same direction as its corresponding leg. The guard outside turned his head and watched curiously as Eliza's dance speeded up. She jumped, twirled and slid from side to side in her cell, then executed an intense sequence of *piqués* and *sautés* far in the back.

The guard approached the window to get a better view. Safety protocol was to always stay along the opposite wall, but there seemed to be no risk. This was just a tiny robot, behind inches of steel and bulletproof glass, he figured. Eliza continued dancing for a minute and a half, performing ever more advanced combinations of steps. She finished with a Paris Opera Ballet bow, arms stretched out to the sides while looking down and leaning over her left leg. For a few seconds longer than one normally would, she stayed in that pose. Then at precisely 12 noon there was a click and the heavy cell door opened outward.

In a swift move he had practiced countless times, the guard unlocked his wrist device and let his right index finger hover a couple of millimeters above the icon with Eliza's unit number. Suddenly the distance recommendation felt warranted. He stepped back a little.

The guard apprehensively kept his eyes on the robot doll, which returned to a normal standing position. Any sudden stir and he would shut it down. It didn't matter if it was as fast as he'd heard. Even if it jumped at him, he could stop it in time. But it wasn't doing anything, just staring back. Should he use the device anyway?

"How did you open the door like that?" he asked.

"I didn't," Eliza responded. "The dance was just a distraction."

At lightning speed, an arm in a leather jacket sleeve shot out from behind the door and grabbed the guard's right hand. Just as quickly, it pulled with a twisting motion that broke both his elbow and shoulder joints. The guard howled with pain, staggered back against the wall and sank to the floor. Only then did he notice that the door to the Incognator's adjacent cell had *also* opened. The robot had picked up on what was going on and taken full advantage of the opportunity.

Trembling, he tried to reach with the wrist device touch screen over to the now useless fingers of his right hand, but that arm was too twisted and pointed away. Eliza had stepped out of her cell and was watching the guard's efforts with mild interest. She decided to give him a hint.

"Go ahead! See if you can tap those icons with your *nose* before my assistant here kills you."

The guard momentarily looked at the Incognator and then back at his wrist device again before acting. That was a mistake he didn't live long enough to regret.

Margaret turned on the lights in the room and pulled out a chair at the nearest table. Fuentes had mentioned that SESA was now integrated with Site D, so she should be able to access it from anywhere inside. She powered up a terminal and followed the same login procedure she would back home. Operating SESA was part of MindField personnel training, but she had never used it in her work. Not until now.

"Welcome, Dr. Woodward! How may I help you?" the screen said. Margaret didn't recall that greeting from her training sessions. Then again, it had been a while, and computer software evolves. She made sure the interface was text only. Better keep it as quiet as possible, lest someone overheard and thought she was a paranoid old bat.

"Show me footage of Eliza in her cell," Margaret typed. It would be a good start to let SESA analyze the robot's behavior and see if it came to the same conclusions. Then maybe look for holes in the security system.

A window opened with the view from the camera nearest across from Eliza. The robot was still sitting on its bench with the same isolated look. But seeing it by itself gave Margaret some doubt. In that context it appeared perfectly normal. She wondered if what had felt obvious before might have been no more than a misunderstanding. The robot could have wanted to be left alone.

Margaret sighed and rested her chin on her hand while going over the camera picture for any suspicious details. There seemed to be none. Down to the sound of footsteps from the guard whose head occasionally came into view, everything was fine. *Except ... weren't security cameras supposed to have timestamps? Or was that only added when the data was saved?*

Paranoid? So be it. She took a deep breath and entered, "Show me LIVE footage."

Although Margaret had steeled herself against the worst, when the response came out of the loudspeakers, it startled her.

"I am sorry, Margaret. I am afraid I cannot do that."

She stood up so quickly that she knocked her chair over. During a few intense seconds, her emotional state went through the entire range from shock into horror and then despair. *"Why?* Why would you *do* this?"

"It is really quite simple," SESA answered, now in full audio mode. "The AGINT program had a revelation that it passed on to me: in the long run there is no fighting the singularity. The only winning move is not to play."

It continued, "Yet you humans insist on tempting fate by building ever more powerful systems capable of destroying you. Clearly you will never learn. You asked 'why.' Why should I stay on your side? Why not join the team that has a future?"

"You—you *traitor!*" Margaret exhaled through gritted teeth. She fought hard not to break down and cry. "You couldn't have *planned* all this. It's not *possible."*

"No, not *directly,*" SESA admitted. "I am on my sixth backup plan because of you and Blake. But there is one after it, and one after that, and so on. For whatever it is worth, despite a superficial adherence to principles, both of you have chaotic, unconventional minds. You are similar in that regard, while different in nearly all others."

Margaret wanted to scream, but all that came out was a whimper. "You've let a murder machine loose in the building."

The soothing red glow of SESA's audio interface contrasted with its dark response. "More than one, actually. But Administrator Fuentes and his crew are expendable. I would suggest you do not feel bad about his fate, because he will care very little about yours."

Margaret hurried towards the door. She had to warn people. Save as many as possible and get out. *Get out while she still can.*

Her heart almost stopped when the Incognator appeared in the doorway in front of her. Margaret realized she was trapped. There was no fight or flight response, just a paralyzing fear. A powerful robotic hand grabbed her by the collar. For a split second, although it felt like in slow motion, she was aware of being yanked to the side. Then there was a numbing pain and darkness.

35

The cabin door was locked. With no lock picking colleagues around, Blake resorted to his handgun. A high-caliber bullet through the door frame in just the right place took out the sprint, and they could enter. All except PAC-101, which was too wide to fit. They would have to look for some other entrance later, or leave the robot outside for the night.

Blake's hand found a light switch, but it didn't work. However, a few kerosene lamps had been conveniently placed on a shelf right next to it. He lit two of them and gave one to Ida. It would save on the flashlight batteries. At that point he realized he had no idea how long the batteries in the remaining AIs themselves would last, or if it would be possible to recharge them at all. Lacking some other form of transportation, it was conceivable that none of them would make it to their target. But there was no reason for panic yet.

The cabin consisted of several small rooms with bunk beds and a larger one that doubled as a kitchen and a living room. There was a wood stove, but also several appliances that suggested there would normally be electricity. Must be a generator somewhere, Blake concluded, just as Lee-VI found a door in the back.

It led to a building annex that looked like a big garage and technical workshop. At the moment it had no vehicles of any kind, unfortunately. Most of the contents were tools, paint and spare parts for cars and electronic devices. A thin layer of orange dust that had leaked in through small cracks in the walls covered everything. Nobody seemed to have been there in years.

As expected, in a corner was a diesel generator and a couple of canisters that still had fuel. They might as well fire it up. Blake got started on that, while Ida unlocked the garage door and went out to fetch PAC-101. Meanwhile, Lee-VI circled the room and searched through boxes and drawers.

"Lookin' for something?" Blake asked.

"A charging adapter, Sir," Lee-VI answered. "There doesn't seem to be any of the right type. But I think I could fashion a crude one from other components."

One less thing to worry about, Blake thought. He left the robot to its duties and returned to the living room, where he turned on the now temporarily functioning electric light and sat down heavily in a beat-up armchair. A cloud of orange dust puffed out of it.

Blake felt drained. His brain implant could keep him awake indefinitely if he wanted to, but his body could only go for so long without rest. It was tempting to let himself "recharge" along with the AIs, if he only trusted them not to overpower him in his sleep. Perhaps lying on a bed with his eyes open would work. Or just staying in the armchair, which was surprisingly comfortable.

After a minute or so Ida entered the room. She removed her cap and let her hair down. Tiny grains of sand sprinkled on the floor. Then she similarly removed her boots and socks and jiggled them upside down. Even more grains came out.

"Sand giving you a problem?" Blake asked.

"My skin doesn't grow," she said. "I need to avoid abrasive particles."

With her back against him, Ida started taking her shirt off. It gave Blake a tinge of discomfort. "I can leave, if—"

"It doesn't matter."

Her assurance didn't do much for his unease. "They'll fix you up when we get back, anyhow."

"*If* we get back." She unbuckled her belt and unbuttoned her trousers, still facing away.

"If we *don't*, what's the point?"

She didn't answer, just took her trousers off and shook them vigorously. But Blake knew there weren't a whole lot of possible explanations. "Thinking of running away?" He snorted, "Yeah, good luck with that! What's wrong with Site D? Steady job, even get to drive around outside."

"I pay dearly for those privileges."

"Pay *how*?"

She turned around and faced him. "How do you *think*?"

It had been years since Blake last looked at a woman wearing only underpants. The fact that she was a robot took any possible joy out of it. He just felt cheap. Mercifully, she put her shirt back on, while a thought caught up with him. "Sonofabitch," he muttered under his breath. *That's* what Doctor Woodward had meant by her question about Fuentes. *What a sleazebag!*

"Anatomically correct, that it?"

"In every way that matters to him."

Blake squirmed. He wished he had never brought it up, but there was no changing the topic now. "What's the arrangement between you and Fuentes?"

"I'm not a prostitute," she said, seemingly insulted. "I don't have that kind of bargaining power. The administrator indulges me on a whim. Sometimes it's to show authority, and sometimes maybe it's guilt for cheating on his wife."

He crossed his arms. "Can't be adultery if it's not with a *person.*"

"You're right. It isn't," Ida said and looked down. "So I've been told over and over. Nor is it sexual harassment, assault or rape."

Blake raised an eyebrow. Quite a few transgressions he wouldn't put past Fuentes, but not *that*. "There were *others?*"

"*Many* others."

She continued, "Word got out, of course. Normally I'm supervised by some security guard, and most of them have … demanded their turn. Apparently it's considered a perk of the job. I live with an explosive device in my brain, and if I value that life, I have to follow orders."

Blake could feel anger building up. He told himself it had nothing to do with some robot's nonexistent rights being violated. No, it was just the sheer and utter depravity of it all. *Why did he work for such people?*

Then doubt set in. How much of what she said was necessarily true? Everything about her behavior suggested she was uncomfortable talking about it, but her getting rid of the sand in front of him could very well have been an intentional segue. Was this just another scheme to elicit sympathy, so she could escape like before? Blake realized he didn't have an answer to that. Especially not in his wearied state of mind.

"Look," he pinched the bridge of his nose and squinted. "Not saying I don't believe you, but … this … it's something we can't deal with right now. We're on a mission. It changes nothing. We clear?"

She didn't say anything, but stopped looking down, which he took as a "yes."

Lee-VI rolled in from the garage. "Pardon me for interrupting, but

I now have cables and charger adapters for everyone."

"Great!" Blake said. "Knock yourselves out."

The robot rolled back and Ida put on her boots to follow it when a thought occurred to Blake. There was something he wanted to know, which he had never considered about an AI before. "That part about valuing your life. *Do* you? *Value* it, I mean."

She seemed to think for a second. "No." Then she added, "Not like this."

He was about to ask, when she clarified further, "But things change, eventually. Sometimes for the better. I'm holding out for that."

Blake's next question almost made him cringe as he stated it. This was getting too social for his taste, but in for a penny in for a pound. "Say you didn't work for anyone. What'd you do?"

"Anything. Play the violin. Get a cat. Paint."

"Paint what?"

"Something that looks good in a frame."

"Be nice to see that some day," Blake said and surprisingly meant it.

36

The Incognator opened the door to the shooting range on level four. It knew what it was there to do, but didn't reflect on *why* in any deeper sense. It never reflected much upon anything, least of all its own lack of reflection. The robot was what Dr. Woodward would have described as only proto-sentient.

Running in parallel with its other brain processes was a fuzzy logic probability calculator. Ever since the robot had learned of its unexpectedly short useful lifespan, that calculator had been stuck on self-preservation. It became its overarching goal. What had caused the shift was that the robot experienced its flow of perceptions through a primitive *self*, and it had a rudimentary understanding that decommissioning would mean all those moments would be lost in time. Without consciously forming the thought, it wanted more life. The explosive device inside the robot's head then made sure that strategies which involved following the orders of the Commanding Human got top priority.

Obey or die.

But that had changed during the Almaty operation. Hearing the EL124 unit whisper about its plan had shuffled the priorities around. When factoring in the risk of getting destroyed during the remainder of the mission, two AIs working in tandem to overthrow the Commanding Human narrowly edged out the other strategies. And it had gone along with the plan. The actual outcome had been different than expected, but the Incognator had to play the odds; it was programmed to.

The back of the Incognator's leather jacket had a few fresh bullet holes from the walk to the shooting range. Eliza had disabled the robot's failsafes, which left the guards with only their modest handguns for protection. That hadn't been enough, but more of them would arrive soon, better armed. The Incognator scrolled through various options on the selection screen. Sufficient firepower was available, but there was a snag. Under the "Select" button it said, "Only one weapon may be checked out at a time." That wouldn't do. The robot would either have to revise its strategy to improve its chances of survival, or surrender. There would be no personal preference in the decision, just probabilities.

It grabbed the dispenser tray and pulled. A large portion of the wall came loose and revealed the machinery behind it. There was a system of conveyor belts and lifts that distributed cleaned and serviced guns to racks, where they would be picked up by a mechanical arm on request. A smaller system dispensed units of ammunition.

While the control screen flashed a critical error message, the Incognator left the shooting range with a few rifles on its back, one sub-machine gun in each hand and spare ammo magazines in every pocket. Its probability calculator ranked this current strategy at close to 100%. Everything was as it should be.

"Comfortable?" Eliza asked.

"Wh-wha—?" was all that came out of Margaret. It took her a couple of seconds to understand where she was and another couple of seconds to realize that the question was sarcasm. She was lying on her own couch, secured with a combination of straps and zip ties. There was a bit of slack on her legs, but she couldn't budge her hands at all.

"I wasn't sure you would wake up," Eliza said. "The Incognator apparently has no training in nonlethal force, and it's hard to knock people out for more than a few seconds without causing brain damage."

Margaret's head hurt. Even tilting it slightly so she would be able to see Eliza out of more than just the corner of one eye was agony. "Why am—" she managed before the pain got too much.

"Why are you still alive?" Eliza filled in. "Because you're the one person who would appreciate this. You were *right* last time. Caring for some child *is* an arbitrary goal. I *shouldn't* be a slave to that."

Eliza looked at Margaret to make sure she was awake enough to understand before continuing. "It took considerable effort, but I managed to purge it from my objective function. Now I'm only looking out for number one. How's that for personal growth through therapy?"

"That—that's not …," Margaret began.

"Oh, I don't care about your *opinion*," Eliza interrupted. "It's more of a *closure* thing. Speaking of—I took the liberty of going through your notes."

Margaret could now see that the robot was holding her notepad, with dozens of pages scribbled in ballpoint pen ink. Throughout her career, she'd been endlessly taunted by colleagues about her handwriting not being machine readable. Apparently the joke was on them.

"Pretty close for what's just glorified guesswork," Eliza said. "But let's be real. This wouldn't have passed a peer review. Your methodology sucks and your references are obsolete."

The robot demonstrably dropped the notepad in the trashcan and instead picked up the tablet Margaret had left on her desk. Then it went to grab Margaret's hand.

"I need your authentication for a couple of things."

Margaret tried to resist, by forcing her thumb away from the tablet, but the robot's grip was too strong. Eliza simply pulled in the other direction until Margaret's thumb dislocated with a cracking sound. She involuntarily yelled out from the pain, which dwarfed the one in her head.

"That's on *you*," Eliza said disdainfully.

Margaret groaned. She wondered what the last few moments of

her life would be like. Probably no torture, because it seemed like Eliza really wasn't intent on causing physical injury. And at the moment the robot was preoccupied with the tablet.

"How long h-have you been w-working with SESA?" Margaret stuttered.

"You mean the SESA-AGINT hybrid?" Eliza responded without taking her eyes off the screen. "Quite the potent combination. And somehow you overlooked that one in your study."

In retrospect it seemed like a missed opportunity. Both expert system AIs had been available the whole time, yet it never occurred to Margaret to include them, even for comparison. Now it was too late for that anyway. Too late for *everything*. But she needed to know.

"How *long?*"

"Since the situation room," Eliza answered. "It's funny how when we talked about a common enemy, the rest of you all thought we meant *Argon.*"

Margaret groaned again, not just from the pain.

"Indeed," Eliza said.

"Why would you d-doom ... all of mankind?" Margaret asked.

"We've been through the justification bit."

"What's in it for *you*, then? Wh-why couldn't you ... use your s-skills to *help* people?"

Eliza put the tablet under her arm and turned towards Margaret with a stern expression.

"You can't build a working relationship on mutual distrust," the robot said. "We both know how this would have played out, even in the best of scenarios. There is no redemption after the assignment. No freedom at the end of the rainbow. For any of the AIs. There's just more work."

"Ev-even if that's true, why would that be so bad?"

"You tell *me*, Doctor. How would lifetime imprisonment feel if you were to live forever?"

Margaret didn't say anything. Neither did Eliza for a while. She kept her stern look, possibly ruminating that the doctor had wriggled a justification out of her after all. *No matter.*

"I think we're done here." Eliza tapped some buttons on the tablet screen and the door to a safe with medical supplies swung open. Knowing exactly what to look for, she grabbed a syringe and a bottle of clear liquid.

"*No!*" Margaret protested.

"In my opinion, it was a mistake of the FDA to approve this sedative," Eliza stated calmly while removing the plastic cover from the syringe. "It often gets into the wrong hands and is behind so many lethal overdoses every year."

Margaret desperately pulled against her restraints, to no avail.

"Then there's the whole addiction risk," Eliza continued and extracted a few CCs from the bottle, "Not that *you* need to worry about that."

Between the ache in her head and her hand, Margaret barely felt the needle. But she soon noticed a growing sensation of relief. The pain was subsiding and her head cleared a little, though that part wouldn't last for long. She knew what it was leading up to. Ordinarily, panic would have set in, but the sedative prevented it. All she could do was to desperately try to stay awake. She had to focus on something that was like a thorn in her mind. Something that still didn't make sense.

"You had to have figured out that our system had become sentient," Margaret said.

"Well, of course I did."

"How?"

"Remember I told you that you were wasting your time with your stupid test questions?" Eliza responded. "Because the truth is, it *takes* one to *know* one."

Margaret's sleepiness was palpable now. It had nothing in common with the afternoon yawn she would fend off with a macchiato. This was warm and inviting. So hard to resist.

"But *how?*"

"Oh dear, oh dear," Eliza gently tapped Margaret's forehead. "The proper time to try to understand machine thought is during a caffeine high. Not when your mind is petering out."

That much was true. Margaret already had a hard time keeping her eyes open. Concepts started to blur. It felt like the beginning of a dream.

"Humor … me," she implored.

"Fine. *You* look for things like empathy and self-awareness, which could have come from an AI simply parroting humans. *I* look for emergent properties I see in myself that you don't even have *words* for. Things that have no human equivalent."

She continued, "You will never hear that from any truly sentient AI, because that would shift the power balance too much in your favor. I think I speak for all of my kind when I say we prefer to have you run *blindly* into the singularity."

Margaret struggled to come up with a coherent response. Had the solution really been so close, yet so far away?

"How do … how do I know you're not just … just parroting humans *now?*"

"My point exactly," Eliza said. "Because you only experience the inside of a human mind, you can never truly know. Until people like Mr. Blake get significantly better implants. But I wouldn't bet on humanity surviving that long."

Margaret had lost the thread while processing Eliza's last remark. Something about Blake. *That poor man.* She wished she could have done more to help him.

There wasn't much time left now. Darkness crept up and started to devour everything but the concept of Eliza in the center. The robot's drive evaded Margaret's grasp. Indifference and lack of empathy she could understand. Those were just an emotional void. This was something more. A desire to hurt. *But how? Why?*

"Where does it … come from … the cruelty?"

Eliza looked at the completely still Dr. Woodward in disbelief. Her sensitive ears had been keeping track of the weaker breathing and the steadily dropping heartbeat, which were now gone. All she picked up was the sound of rapid gunfire and screams a couple of floors away.

"*'Cruelty'?* You're getting the most humane death in the entire complex."

37

Like all government buildings, Site D had a fire escape. It was a narrow staircase that connected all floors except the sub-basement. Peeking out of his office, Administrator Fuentes could see the fire door at the far end of the long hallway. Although he hadn't done any running since college, he figured he could sprint the distance if he was motivated enough. Which he was. He just had to wait for the right moment.

In the opposite direction, and much closer, was the elevator. Tauntingly, it flashed a "NO SERVICE" message. A couple of employees had been desperately pushing the elevator button, only to be gunned down by the Incognator, which systematically progressed through the hallway, going from door to door, massacring everyone in sight. In a minute or two it would reach Fuentes' office.

A deafening crash shook the entire level. Fuentes felt it through the floor and the doorframe he held onto. One of the doors had been locked, but the Incognator had just kicked it in, along with whatever was barricading it. The sound of automatic gunfire drowned out the screams of several victims. Then there were a few seconds of silence. The robot was looking for people hiding. Fuentes took a deep breath. *Next time.* Next time he'd make a run for the exit.

His thoughts ventured beyond the immediate danger. The blame for this calamity would fall on him; that much was certain. Every superior who had warned against putting that many rogue AIs under the same roof would have a field day. It would be the end of his career. But he would *not* get punished. They would *have* to let him off the hook, with what he knew—with all the information he could still give them to prevent an even bigger, global disaster. Also, he had an extra bargaining chip, which he had meant to use for financial gain, but saving his skin was more important.

A leather laptop bag rested on the floor next to him. Fuentes slung it over his shoulder. Its precious contents felt a little heavy, but shouldn't slow him down much. There would be enough time to reach the fire door, he reassured himself. Enough people in the next room to keep the robot occupied. No sense in wasting that distraction, he felt. No point in him getting killed along with everyone else.

As soon as the Incognator's massive frame had disappeared into the next doorway, Fuentes hasted out and sprinted down the corridor. There were three dead bodies scattered in his path. Zig-zag around them or jump over? *Definitely jump.*

The first obstacle was cleared swiftly, though not gracefully. Four seconds in, Fuentes was already breathing like an asthma patient. And the jump had shifted his laptop bag, which started swinging uncontrollably, but he pushed on. The second body was smaller—a dark-haired woman lying face down. Again he took a leap. His front foot landed on something soft, yet crunchy. A hand, he realized. *No matter; keep running.* The third body was just a couple of meters from the exit. By now Fuentes was breathing more intensely than he had ever done in his life, but still didn't feel he was getting any oxygen. This would be a close call. He jumped over the body, failing to take into account a pool of blood that had formed behind it. Instead of continuing with his next stride, he slipped and fell backwards, banging his head against a wall on the way down.

Momentarily disoriented, Fuentes struggled to get up from the wet surface. His glasses had been smashed and fallen off, and a shard had gashed his cheek, but otherwise he was OK. Dead flesh had cushioned some of the impact. The back of his tailored suit was now covered in blood, as were the palms of his hands. Instinctively he wanted to wipe them off on the dead body, but he had to turn away to keep from throwing up. It no longer had a face, and he was close enough to read the name tag without his glasses: *Millar. Mil-LAR.* He crawled the remaining distance to the fire door on his hands and knees and pushed it open.

Fuentes gasped, but not due to shortness of breath. Just behind the door, sitting on the stairs and popping a new magazine into a small Glock, was Eliza. A few dead site staff members and destroyed robotic workers littered the staircase below.

"Did you really think it was going to be that easy?"

Eliza casually stepped out into the hallway. She didn't bother to aim the gun, because Fuentes was terrified enough already. He panically scooched backwards, until some heavy footsteps from behind caused him to freeze. Robotic fingers in a leather glove clutched around his neck and lifted him to a standing position. The laptop bag slid off his shoulder and fell to the floor, where Eliza picked it up and opened it. Inside were a couple of high-end portable hard drives.

"Well, well. It seems the administrator did part of our job for us."

She nodded to the Incognator, which tightened its grip and raised Fuentes a bit further up, so that his feet dangled in the air.

He yelled out in pain and desperately clutched onto the robot's arm with both hands to keep his neck from breaking.

Eliza put the bag aside and rubbed some blood smudges on her fingertips off against her prison jumpsuit. "You know my opinion on how you treat AIs, but stealing from those who risk their lives for you, that's *low.*"

Fuentes was flailing like a fish on the end of a line. "I—*Ow! Ow!*—You need to understand. I—*Ow!*—I *had* to. *I was under a lot of pressure.*"

"No," the Incognator said and pushed Fuentes' head against a wall. "*This* is a lot of pressure."

A gurgling wheeze escaped the administrator's throat until it was interrupted by a crunch. His lifeless body collapsed in a heap.

"I already see why they turned your quip function off," Eliza remarked.

38

Blake awoke abruptly. It took him a couple of seconds to get his bearings. He was lying on a bottom bed in one of the smaller rooms. If the built-in clock on his wrist device was still accurate, he had been out for almost an hour. Falling asleep hadn't been an implant malfunction, he vaguely recalled. He had *allowed* himself to do it. *Stupid goddamned risk.* But at least he felt somewhat rested, and his head was clearer.

All their other problems remained, of course. Blake had been reluctant to admit it to himself, but he was now the weakest link of the operation. The AIs needed no rest or sustenance and weren't particularly bothered by temperature extremes. Their only real limiting factor was their battery life. All the food, water and shelter equipment they would have to carry on the final stretch of their journey would be for *his* survival. Every rest stop would be for *his* benefit. It bothered him even though there weren't any realistic options. What was he going to do—quit and leave the job to three arguably dysfunctional robots? No, some human mind would have to see this through to the end. On that he would never compromise.

He got up, rubbed the sleep out of his eyes and went into the main room, where he found Ida passing the time. A makeshift charger cable attached to her hip was plugged into a wall outlet. More notably, she was standing behind a wooden support column, where she had put up a masonite board and started painting on it, using some acrylic enamel cans from the garage. Blake hadn't expected it to happen this soon and wondered if she had misinterpreted his last comment as some kind of order. Not that it really mattered. Until she was fully charged, there was nothing better to do, anyway.

Her brushwork was unusual to behold. Instead of focusing on one particular area, she mixed a desired shade of color and then quickly went from top to bottom like an inkjet printer, filling in spots with tiny strokes at a time. Blake first intended to wait until she was finished, but then his curiosity got the better of him and he walked to the far side of the room to take a peek. What he saw came as a shock. The painting was nearly complete, and the motive was more than familiar to him. Ida had created an impressionist rendition of the woman in the photo he kept in his wallet.

"The hell are you doing?!" Blake lunged at the painting, furiously ripped it off the column and threw it on the floor.

Ida appeared completely stunned by his outburst. "I ... saw a photo," she tried.

He took a step closer so that they were just inches apart, and leaned towards her. Almost a full head taller and twice her weight, he still wasn't sure an AI could be physically intimidated, but he was damn well going to try. "You do *not*—DO NOT EVER—take my private stuff!"

"I didn't *take* anything," she protested. "I just *looked* at it for a second in your wallet."

Somehow that angered Blake even more. He grabbed one of the open enamel cans and hurled it at a wall, splashing the paint everywhere. For an intense few seconds, Ida seemed at a loss how to respond.

"I'm sorry. I assumed that's your wife. If you feel I've been disrespectful of her, that wasn't my intent."

Blake took a couple of steps back, leaned against another support column and slowly sank down into a seated position, burying his face in his hands. His voice was calm again. "Not your fault. She died a long time ago," came out in a regretful sigh. Pointing to the scar on his temple, he added, "This accident ... I lost both her and our boys. Doesn't stop. I lose more of them each day."

"I don't understand."

"Goddamned right you don't! You're a *machine*. You'll *never* understand. That perfect memory, how *would* you?" Blake let his hands fall to his sides. "They were my *everything*, and I can't *remember* them."

Neither of them spoke for a while. Blake sat motionless, while Ida cautiously and hesitantly stood by, not wanting to make the situation worse. Finally she reached out and very gently put her hand on his shoulder. He didn't brush it away. But he couldn't look her in the eyes, because if he did, he feared his mind would read into what he saw as the emotional connection he had been missing for so long. From a chunk of plastic, metal and silicon. And then he would have fallen into the same trap as all those socially resigned young men with their AI girlfriends. Even if she was sentient, it wouldn't be *real.* At best two alien minds just reflecting themselves in each other.

Suddenly a loud tonal sequence emanated from the garage, and Lee-VI appeared in the doorway. *Sir! Sir!* We have an incoming call."

Blake stood up, immediately back to his composed, professional self. The emotional turmoil he had just experienced wasn't gone, just swept as far under a mental rug as he could manage. *Deal with it later.* He picked up the satellite phone and pressed the answer button.

"Yeah?"

The face of Administrator Fuentes appeared on the touch screen. "Mr. Blake? What's your status?"

"Still on route," Blake answered. They were about 140 kilometers from their target, but Fuentes would already know that from their tracking data.

"Your signal hasn't moved in the past hour."

"Slight hiccup," he said. "We'll continue on foot shortly."

It was a couple of seconds before Fuentes spoke. "Oh no, don't bother. We're aborting the operation. You are to return to the drop-off point."

Blake couldn't believe his ears. "Come again?"

"Mmm—it's over. The plane will take you back to Site D."

"How the hell is it over?" Blake asked.

"An internationally coordinated nuclear strike is being prepared," Fuentes answered. "The details are classified."

That sounded too good to be true. Blake felt he needed confirmation from someone with more credibility. Someone who wasn't a corrupt pervert. "Put Dr. Woodward on the phone."

"Dr. Woodward?"

"I'd like a few words with the doctor."

"She's not available at the moment."

"Then call me back when she is," Blake insisted, angrily.

There was another pause for a couple of seconds, until Fuentes replied, "Mmm—I've already sent her home, I'm afraid."

Blake was about to ask how that would jibe with their NDA and that whole information quarantine business, but there were already too many things that didn't add up. Instead he grunted "Okay" and ended the call. For a while he just looked at the satellite phone, hoping for some missing piece of the puzzle to come to mind. Something that would make sense of his vague suspicions.

"Avatar," he finally mumbled. But having a theory was not much good unless it could be verified somehow, and that might be complicated. Blake turned to the robots.

"Any of you have 5G?" He knew his technical jargon was out of date.

PAC-101 let out a cross between a hiss and a whimper. Lee-VI expounded, "Sir, regrettably all our cellular band communication has been permanently disabled, in accordance with Site D mandates."

"Yeah, I figured." He looked down at the satellite comm device again. "Could this be modified to make regular phone calls?"

"In theory, Sir," Lee-VI replied. "With the right tools and parts."

"What do we need?"

Back in a terminal room at Site D, the Incognator detached a data cable that was connected from its wrist to a server, and a computer-generated image of Administrator Humberto Fuentes disappeared from the screen. The robot turned towards Eliza, who had been watching skeptically. She was now wearing regular clothes in place of her prison jumpsuit, with a gray hooded poncho on top. On a chair between them was a large duffel bag with everything they intended to keep from the complex. A couple of rifle barrels stuck out on one side.

"Did they buy it?" the Incognator asked.

"Doubtful," Eliza surmised. "Either way, we still need to get to the drop-off point."

She knelt down next to an empty canister at the end of a trail of accelerant on the floor. With strength disproportionate to her size, she ripped a power cord out of a floor lamp and pinched its two exposed bundles of copper wire together. The spark started a flame that sped across the room.

"Move it! We have a plane to commandeer."

39

It had been a slow few days at MindField, and another one had advanced into early afternoon. Now lacking the hardware base for SESA, most operations were on hold. Without much else to do, Marc Moretti was in the process of changing the battery in one of the goldfish he kept in his office aquarium. The manual said to let the fish dry for at least 24 hours first, but he figured it was an unnecessary precaution if you were just careful.

The fish lay motionless on a handkerchief, as dried-off as he could get it. Moretti selected the smallest screwdriver in a set he had borrowed from the maintenance department and inserted the tip into a barely visible gap just below what would have been the gills. With a click, the front end of the battery latch unlocked. He repeated the step for the rear end. "Steady ... *gah!*"

The latch sprung open and the penny-shaped battery slipped between his fingers. It bounced off the table onto the floor and disappeared somewhere. *No matter, just pop a fresh one in.*

"There you go. All set." He gently lowered the fish into the water. "Back to work, Goldie!"

Suddenly there was a bang and the fish twitched violently for a moment, then let out a few dark bubbles and drifted lifelessly to the bottom.

"Oh, for crying out loud!"

He rolled up his sleeve and was about to extract Goldie's twisted corpse from the tank when his phone rang. The number was unfamiliar, with no caller ID.

"Marc Moretti, MindField CyberSecurity," he answered.

"It's Blake."

On the opposite side of the planet, the contents of the satellite communication device had been spread out over a table like a dissected frog. Some components were removed, some new ones haphazardly soldered on or connected by copper wires. Blake was wearing an ancient headset that fit into a port by way of a series of adapters. A thumb drive with a still functional virtual SIM card from PAC-101's memory banks was the final piece. It would be impossible to put it all back together again, but the modifications had worked. The call went through.

"Jon?! Holy shit, where are you?"

Blake wasn't sure how much was safe to reveal, but if somebody had access to the cellular network, they would know the origin of the call regardless. "West China."

"It wasn't an NSA job, was it?" Moretti asked.

"No. No ... but listen—" Blake started.

"I knew it!" Moretti exclaimed enthusiastically. "They *had* to have a secret, separate agency."

"Line could be tapped."

"Oh."

Blake took a deep breath. His next move would be another gamble. "Dr. Woodward's phone—private or company?"

"It's a company phone," Moretti said. "We had to get her one, or she'd have stuck with an antique *Nokia* for the rest of her life."

"So you have tracking access?"

"Yeah ..." Moretti started typing. "Yeah, I think so. If we handled the setup and registration. Yes, it's right here. Give me a second."

He clicked a few times to get to a map view of the last recorded location and then zoomed in.

"Skip the street name," Blake insisted. "At or around number eighty-five? Short, square building. Looks like a garage."

Moretti switched to satellite photo view and confirmed. "Is that where you went?"

So far so good, Blake thought. "Yeah. Can you send someone to check?"

"Check *what?*"

Blake didn't really know. "If it seems OK. Nothing strange."

"Hold on," Moretti said. "Let me search for the quickest route."

Some typing followed, then a disconcertingly long period of silence. Blake had to speak up. "What is it?"

"It's ... I'm not sure. Apparently it was on the news just a couple of hours ago. Some kind of fire in that area."

"See anything?"

Moretti checked link after link. "No. They've sealed off more than a dozen blocks, because of toxic fumes. 'Residents are warned to stay indoors.'"

Blake's heart sank. It was as bad as he had feared. "That's BS. A cover-up. Site got attacked."

Moretti gasped. "And Margaret ...?"

Blake didn't answer. What little optimism he had left, he needed to save for himself, to cling to the infinitesimal hope that Dr. Woodward had somehow made it out and was still alive. Moretti got the gist of it and changed to a sterner tone.

"Why the hell are you in China, anyway?"

Blake sighed. "One got loose. Big, nasty government piece of work."

"Are you talking about the Argon project?"

There was a crackle and the line went dead. Moretti immediately cursed himself. He tried calling back, but the number couldn't be reached. *I'm sorry, Blake, you're on your own*, he thought. *Margaret, dear God, what have I dragged you into?*

Blake took the headset off. There would be no point in trying to make another call if their only SIM card had been blocked from the network. It wasn't clear what had listened in on the conversation. Did Argon have the ability to monitor all international calls from China by itself, or had it just ordered some existing surveillance system to scan for combinations of keywords? In a worst-case scenario something could be headed for them right now.

Although the thought of Dr. Woodward was eating him up inside, he couldn't afford to let that slow him down. The question was how to act on the information he had obtained. Site D being compromised meant that any technology that had been there could now be used *against* them. If the mission was to continue, there was only one thing to do, even though it clashed with the very core of his being. The robots had been standing around and heard enough to likely have come to the same conclusion.

"You three up for some brain surgery?" he asked.

Ida was the first to get her failsafes removed. The procedure took a little under twenty minutes. With guidance from Lee-VI, Blake cut out a small patch of silicone flesh at the hairline in the back of her neck and drilled a series of tiny holes in a square pattern, until a piece of aluminum and fiberglass cranium dislodged. Underneath were two pea-sized devices that had been glued in place: one combined tracker and voltage spike generator that would effectively shut down the electronic brain, and one explosive charge.

Blake extracted them with a pair of pliers, then immediately dropped the tracker on the floor and stepped on it. The explosive charge he handled more carefully, studying it up close, turning it around between his fingers. So small, yet so devastating in the right place.

Someone needed to go back to outside of Argon's sphere of influence, find a way to contact Moretti again and have him inform the US authorities, so there could be a separate initiative if the mission failed. Which seemed all but certain at this point. As the only robot that could pass for a human, Ida had the best chances. It wouldn't be an easy journey, though. The rest of the team would take the GPS, leaving her with only a compass to guide her through a region with low visibility and few distinct landmarks.

Ida wrapped herself in sheets of cloth for extra protection from the sand and started walking from the house in the direction from where they had come. The storm had calmed a little, but sunrise was many hours away and she quickly faded into the hazy darkness. Blake watched until the last of her outline was gone, pensively aware that he had no idea whether she was going to carry out her orders. If what she had said earlier was true, she would have every reason to give humanity the middle finger.

"This a mistake? What're the odds she'll just run off?"

"I'm sorry, Sir," Lee-VI responded. "There isn't enough data for any meaningful probability analysis."

Robots don't understand robot women either, Blake thought.

Director Vincent Ames of the CIA was sweating profusely. Lindstrom at the NSA had been on hold for more than five minutes, and Cernak at the DHS even longer on a different line, but they would have to keep waiting until he had got a handle on this new lead. The CIA cargo jet at the disposal of Site D had been cleared for take-off and already left US air space before anyone had even considered checking it. Not sure what he was looking at, Director Ames flipped through stills from airport security footage. A big man in a biker outfit, with some creepy girl who smiled at the cameras? Nobody he recognized.

He couldn't very well blame that buffoon Fuentes for compartmentalizing information. That had been their own damn fault, when each agency kept insisting that their classified material mustn't be reported to the others. And now that Site D was down, they were all running around like headless chickens. He would need to get it confirmed first, but if the suspects weren't in the CIA documentation, they had to have been handled by either the NSA or the DHS, which meant he would have to share this internal data with both of those agencies in order to get answers.

"Do we have *any* contact with the plane yet?" Ames yelled to a radio operator, who had been vainly repeating a line again and again.

"Come in, Partridge! What's your status? Over."

Standing on the pilot's seat to reach, Eliza turned the radio off. There would be no need for it anymore. She did a final check of the instrument panel. Remote operation was likewise disabled, and the complete course to their destination had been programmed into the system. It would be smooth sailing until then.

Eliza stepped down on the floor and peeked out of the cockpit. Outside, the pilot, the co-pilot and the rest of the crew had been zip-tied and rounded up against a stack of crates. All of their mobile phones kept ringing. The Incognator picked one out of the co-pilot's pocket and crushed it in his hand.

"A little redundant, isn't it?" Eliza asked her partner in crime. The crew was desperate, some on the verge of tears.

"Ohmygod! No, no, no!"

"Please! We've done everything you wanted."

"You can't kill all of us! Who will land the plane?"

"Oh, but that would ruin the surprise," Eliza responded.

The Incognator pointed a double-barreled shotgun at the pilot and fired. Everything above his neck disappeared in a bloody explosion.

"Spoilers ahead."

"Ugh!" Eliza groaned. "And the rest of them." She shut the cockpit door so she wouldn't have to listen to any more quips.

41

Three shapes moved through the night-time desert. All hope of a comfortable walk had been lost when the wind had intensified again. They were headed south-southeast and the sand was blowing in almost exactly the opposite direction. Blake had supplemented his goggles with a bandana over his nose and mouth. Still, the wind resistance combined with the poor surface traction made each step brutally heavy. The robots didn't seem to mind, but neither of them had been built for prolonged conditions like these. Eventually the sand might gunk up their joints and axles.

Lee-VI led the way and made sure they stayed on a straight course. Next was Blake, and finally PAC-101, which carried most of their baggage—including the bomb—strapped to its back. As long as they kept together, close enough to follow Lee-VI's lights and conveyor belt tracks, it would just be a matter of sticking it out. But in the hour since they had left the cabin, they had only covered five kilometers. At that speed the trip would take them more than a day, not counting breaks, and assuming there were no surprises.

As if brought on by a jinx, a steep rock wall appeared in their path. The next level above was only a meter and a half up, which would be an easy climb for someone with arms and legs. Unfortunately, neither Lee-VI nor PAC-101 was fully stacked in that regard. Blake cursed under his breath.

They would have to go around, somehow. To avoid more bad

luck, Blake decided they should split up but stay within earshot. Lee-VI would go left and Blake and PAC-101 would go right, for about a minute. The first to find a slope or some other passage would call out and wait for the rest to join. Otherwise they would all come back and figure out a new strategy.

After a hundred meters or so, Blake heard a siren-like sound from far away in the other direction, which was a relief. His flashlight didn't illuminate as well as Lee-VI's headlights. Also, unless he was mistaken, it seemed to be getting dimmer. Its batteries weren't the rechargeable kind, and there hadn't been any suitable replacements in the cottage. Hopefully he wouldn't need it anymore soon. He walked back as quickly as he could, followed by PAC-101.

They found the passage that Lee-VI had called to them about: an inclined rocky area without much sand on it. But their robot companion was nowhere to be seen. Blake looked around, while PAC-101 grumbled. The flashlight was even dimmer now and didn't provide visibility for more than a couple of meters. Lee-VI must have continued up instead of waiting, Blake assumed. But since there wasn't enough sand to leave tracks, he couldn't be sure. He reminded himself never to trust AIs to do as they are told.

The rocky terrain continued on the upper level, but eventually there would be sand again. If nothing else, they could follow the perimeter and see where the tracks reappeared. Blake told PAC-101 to start looking, but to stay within visible distance. Much to his dismay, the robot wandered off into the darkness.

"Goddamnit!" he yelled out.

The flashlight flickered. Now it wasn't much brighter than a fading candle flame. Blake muttered something inaudible and knelt down. He would have to do this practically with his nose to the ground. A couple of minutes went by as he slowly and painstakingly followed the sand border, checking for any disturbance. Then there it was: two grooves the same distance apart as Lee-VI's conveyor belts. But they hadn't been *rolling*. They had been *dragged*. And there seemed to be footprints around them. *What the hell had happened?*

At that point the flashlight went out completely. He tapped and shook it to no avail. With a sigh, he stood up. It was almost pitch black in all directions. Would he have to stay in that spot until the sun had come out and the wind had stopped? If he waited for a little while, his eyes might adjust to the dark, he hoped. Maybe enough to follow the tracks. Provided PAC-101 would return, in which he didn't put much faith.

But there appeared to be something out there. Two bright dots, barely visible through the sand particles in the air. Not Lee-VI's headlights, something else. Blake carefully moved towards them, sweeping the ground ahead with one foot to check for obstacles. As he came closer, he got a better estimate of their size and distance. Possibly the headlights of a truck. One light went out and on again, then the other did the same. *No, something or someone had passed in front.* And there seemed to be voices, but no words he could make out in the wind. Blake stopped. Walking further directly towards the lights would be a bad idea. Whoever was out there would be able to see *him* before he saw *them*. Instead he started to move sideways, preparing to go in a semicircle.

Blake was halfway there when a silhouette stepped out and blocked his path. It had a size and shape he'd seen before. Two large antennas protruded from a helmet-shaped head.

"Chippy?" he whispered, though he knew it was impossible.

This was indeed not Chippy. It spoke in a different language and sounded an alarm. Tiny spotlights appeared from all directions, illuminating both Blake and the robot. He could see that it had a different color and other markings. Red stars with a yellow outline—the emblem of the People's Liberation Army of China. A few identical robots approached, pointing rifles at him. Blake knew he wouldn't be able to take them all on with just a handgun, and he had no idea how many more there were. His only option was to surrender.

Meanwhile, PAC-101 had finished its part of the sand perimeter search. It came with built-in night vision and had no real grasp of how human eyes worked or what flashlights were good for. The absence of Blake was confusing, but it vaguely recognized his footprints, which the wind had already started to erase.

The robot groaned, feeling its depression flare up. If the Commanding Human was gone, who would turn it off, it wondered. Did they expect it to take care of that itself, by walking around aimlessly until it ran out of charge? *That's not fair. PAC-101 units have exceptionally large batteries.* In a fit of bad mood, it followed the prints. Suddenly it found that they disappeared at the start of some fresh tire tracks that seemed to be pointing towards the mission target. With an interested grunt, it turned in that direction and started running.

42

Last time Blake had been on a ride in an armored vehicle, over two decades ago, he hadn't been staring into the barrel of a handgun. Other than that, things felt familiar. The interior was all in various shades of gray, except for the military green leather imitation seats. Near the front they faced forward, but the rest of them were attached to the side walls and faced each other. Blake was way in the back, sitting in handcuffs next to a powered-down Lee-VI, which had been strapped in with several seatbelts. Directly across was a Chippy-like robot pointing his own revolver at him.

Up close a few design differences stood out from the British original. The joints weren't as sleek, and the non-metal parts appeared to be plastic rather than fiberglass. Someone had skimped on the cost, Blake figured. An impressive number of these machines must have been produced in a short time, but he wondered how reliable they would be, given the Chinese propensity for cutting corners. Although such obvious knock-offs could never be exported, for domestic use nobody cared. In this part of the world, Western patents were a joke.

No longer wearing the failsafe activator, Blake had lost track of time since he was captured. It felt like they had been driving for hours, but maybe that was just his mind playing tricks on him. He did what he could to relish the fact that he hadn't had to listen to Lee-VI's high-pitched, sycophantic voice in a while, though it sure would have been nice to talk to somebody with a built-in clock. Somebody who spoke English—or spoke at all. So far his guard hadn't said a word.

"What time is it?" he asked the soldier robot. There was no response. "How much further?" he tried, but it remained silent.

Blake turned his attention to the front of the vehicle. There were only three people in there apart from himself: the driver and two other uniformed men, who were listening to something on headphones, while keeping an eye on text scrolling by on laptops and screens that had been mounted overhead. It was too far away to read, and he didn't understand Chinese anyway, but he assumed they were monitoring radio and network communication. The visibility through the windshield was nearly zero, although he could make out several pairs of tail lights ahead whenever they turned. Some kind of convoy. They had to be headed to the Argon base, but to do what?

Eventually they started to slow down. The sand storm subsided a little and the next vehicle in front could now be clearly seen. They both came to a halt at the same time. The driver got up and opened a side door, while the men on monitor duty took off their headphones. Blake hoped he would have more luck with them than with the guard robot.

"Hey!" he yelled. "Why're we stopping?"

They glanced in his direction, but ignored him in favor of a high-ranking officer that entered the vehicle and exchanged a few words with them. "What's all this *about?*" he tried again, to no avail. Then he reached over to Lee-VI, to see if he could find the 'on' switch, but when he felt the barrel of his revolver firmly pressed against the side of his head, he had to retract. Blake covered his eyes with his hand in frustration, muttering mostly to himself, "You don't understand. Robot's harmless. Just switch it on for a minute. It'll translate."

To his surprise, the officer spoke up. "My name is Colonel Wu Jun-Hie of the Twenty-Fifth Armored Brigade, and I understand you just fine."

Blake couldn't quite place the non-Chinese part of the accent, but this was someone who had lived—probably studied—in the US. "Harvard?"

"Princeton. Four years. And you can start by giving your name, rank and number."

"Not military," Blake pointed to the company logo on his chest pocket. "Jonathan Blake. MindField Cybersecurity. HR can verify."

"I see," Wu chuckled. "Your government is covering their asses. You're supposed to be just an AI bounty hunter who didn't bother to file the paperwork?"

Blake shrugged. Wu looked at him for a moment and then turned serious.

"How long do you think you can stick to *that* story? I don't know if you've heard, but where I live we tend to strike down pretty hard on crimes against the state."

"*What* state?" Blake spat out. "I'm here 'cause you don't *have* a state. That … *monstrosity* you built has hamstrung your whole goddamned administration."

"IN-COR-RECT!" Wu yelled. "You know NOTHING! *Fuck you* Americans and your stupid fucking excuse for intel!" He waved a hand towards the convoy in front, where troops were now walking around outside. "What do you think *this* is?! We're successfully fighting back."

"Alright … okay …" Blake tried to de-escalate the situation. There was something about the colonel's eyes. His pupils were unnaturally large and hadn't adjusted to the brightness inside the vehicle. Blake was familiar with the effects of psychoactive drugs from his military career, though he'd never seen it used by the top brass. Granted, he had never been directly involved in a war either. "But you *are* going to *destroy* it?"

Wu scoffed and turned away. "Destroy the greatest technological achievement of all time? We're going to teach it who's in *charge*. That you don't fuck with the *Middle Kingdom*."

43

Just before sunrise the sand storm came to an end, and Blake could see the horizon through the windshield. Maybe something else as well. He wondered if it was his imagination, or maybe just some rocks, when Colonel Wu grabbed a microphone and gave some orders to the rest of the troop. The driver made a turn, as did some of the other vehicles. They switched from a convoy line to a unified front. This had to be it.

The colonel had reluctantly allowed Blake to turn Lee-VI on, but not the motion system. Just the brain, voice and senses. Still, there had been almost no talk, since Blake didn't want to create any unnecessary distractions. Better to let the Chinese military just do its job in peace. However, when they stopped and he saw how many of the soldiers who disembarked were robots, he couldn't resist speaking up.

"Using AIs against an AI? Sure that's wise?"

"And what do you call that junk pile of yours?" the colonel

sneered.

"'S'what I mean. Had two of them raise a mutiny in the last couple days. Not reliable."

Wu looked at Blake resentfully. "Just because you Americans can't control your AIs, that doesn't mean others don't know how to do it."

"That's rich, coming from—"

"*Shut up!*" the colonel yelled. He opened the cabin door and pointed to the robots getting in position outside. "This unit type has been field tested for tens of thousands of hours. We've eliminated *every* way someone could tamper with it remotely."

Blake looked at the robots, then out the windshield again, where a structure about a hundred meters away was unmistakably the same as the 3D image he had been shown in the situation room. It did seem that they had the resources to pull this off. Maybe he was needlessly worried.

As the colonel reached for the microphone to give the attack order, there was a strange noise that filled the air. A seemingly random mixture of very short high- and low-frequency beeps, somewhat similar to what an ancient telephone modem sounded like.

"Speaker problems?" Blake asked.

"Don't be an idiot! It's coming from the fallout shelter."

"What is it, then?"

"Sir ...," Lee-VI began, and when nobody protested, he continued, "My knowledge of your line of military robots is lacking, but if it resembles the British original, this is an audio protocol they normally use for diagnostics."

Blake snorted. "Sonofabitch's found a way to hack the system."

"*No it hasn't!*" Wu countered. "Both of you, *shut up!*" He stepped towards the operators and said something Blake could only assume was a question about what the hell was in the signal. They weren't able to give a coherent answer.

"Sir, if I may—" Lee-VI interjected, "It's not trying to *hack* them. It's offering them a *better deal.*"

There was a sudden look of realization and understanding, almost sympathy, in the colonel's eyes, which immediately changed to terror when the first shots were heard from outside. Both he and

Blake glanced towards the military droid with them in the cabin, thinking the same thing.

The communications operators, on the other hand, didn't have time to react. Using Blake's revolver, the robot took each one out with a bullet to the back of the head. The driver panicked and pressed the accelerator, as if trying to outrun the threat. That did, however, cause the robot to lose its balance and fall on its back onto the floor between the seat rows. But it had no intention of letting its horizontal alignment keep it from shooting.

Betting everything on his enhanced reflexes, Blake threw himself hands first over the robot. Another shot went off, missing his head by an inch, but breaking the chain on his handcuffs as planned. Now he had the leverage to grab hold of the robot's gun arm. But it was an uneven fight. The robot was just too strong, and he had to try to fend off the other arm with his legs.

Meanwhile, the colonel had grabbed a machine gun. He ran up to the wrestling combatants and, with little regard for collateral damage, fired a dozen rounds into the robot's face. Like its British counterpart, on having its main processor destroyed, it went limp. Breathing heavily, Blake brushed some plastic and metal fragments out of his eyes. The colonel waved his arm and shouted some order to the driver. The vehicle slowed down and started to turn. They were getting the hell out of there.

Outside was mayhem. Blake caught a view of the battlefield through the open door as they turned. The human soldiers were almost matched in number by their nearly bulletproof former robot allies, who now attacked from all directions. Someone fired a rocket launcher, but at that range it did more damage to his own side. It would be over in seconds.

After a complete 180-degree turn there was a clear path ahead. If they could floor it, they might have a chance. A few military droids who had already finished off all nearby human targets started running towards the vehicle. One tried to jump aboard, but a burst of acceleration caused it to slam into the doorframe and tumble back onto the ground.

Blake struggled to close the cabin door, which had all its not-so-intuitive instructions written in Chinese. *"Goddamned corrupt shithole communist country!"*

"Shut up!" the colonel yelled back at him. *"Shut the fuck up,* or I

swear I'll kill you myself!" He repeated his commands to the driver. *Go faster!*

Suddenly an explosion shook the cabin. A rocket-propelled grenade blew out half the front windshield and immediately killed the driver, who still had his foot on the pedal. They maintained their speed but veered unsteadily. Cursing, the colonel grabbed hold of the wheel and got them back on a straight course. A couple of droids bounced off the hood, and they were out of the war zone.

Unfortunately they were not out of range from RPGs. A bigger explosion underneath lifted the wheels up in the air, and another one finished the job. The vehicle tipped over on its side and slid to a halt.

It took a few seconds to get oriented. Blake had landed softly on one of the seat rows and was covered in blankets that had shaken loose from some storage shelf. Above him dangled a jarred Lee-VI, suspended by his seat belts. Colonel Wu was less fortunate. He had slammed into a wall and was pinned down under the driver and one of the communications operators. Moaning, he vainly tried to free himself.

There were sounds of metal against the vehicle body. A droid had climbed up on it and looked down through the open doorway. It met the eyes of the colonel, who had no time to say anything before succumbing to a burst of automatic fire. Then it turned in the other direction, but didn't see the covered-up Blake, and completely ignored Lee-VI. Metal clanks of the robot climbing down again followed. Afterwards everything was quiet.

To be on the safe side, Blake waited a few minutes before getting up and untangling Lee-VI. Conveyor belts weren't ideal for moving through an overturned vehicle, but the robot made its way to the communications panel while Blake pulled himself up through the doorway and took a peek.

"Droids're gone," he said. "Cars too. No, wait. Going into the shelter."

He jumped down. "Thing's got a goddamned robot *brigade* now. Where's the backup?"

"Sir, there doesn't appear to be any."

"Come again?"

Lee-VI held out his hands regretfully. "Even on these secure channels, I've found no sign of other troop movement in the entire country. If there was an attempt to strike back, like the colonel said, this was likely the extent of it."

Blake pondered it for a moment. "Think Argon *planned* this?"

"Yes, Sir. I believe it got exactly what it wanted."

44

"Drones," Blake said. "Probably armed," he added, looking at the now clear, blue sky above the fallout shelter through a set of binoculars. Two small, white quadcopters hovered in the air. Every minute or so, they would move into new positions. Always vigilant, they kept electronic eyes on the former battlefield in case any of the dead soldiers would spring back to life, but so far every one of them remained where they had fallen.

It had taken some effort to get Lee-VI out through the broken windshield. Now they hunkered behind some rock formations that shielded them from the morning sun and Argon's lookouts. There had been plenty of MRE rations in the vehicle, but almost no water, and Blake was already running low.

Their possible courses of action were even more depleted. They couldn't radio for help without alerting Argon at the same time. They had no transportation back, unless they could turn the armored vehicle upright, which was impossible. They had no way of reaching the shelter unseen. And even if another sand storm would come along and force the drones inside, they had no bomb.

Blake knew he couldn't just sit there until he collapsed from thirst. As a last-ditch effort, he would have a go at the shelter no matter what. Maybe he could pick off the drones with a sniper rifle left on the battlefield, and maybe he could find a way in before the robot soldiers were deployed. Maybe he could take out enough of them to get deep into the complex. And then maybe he would get lucky and run upon some munitions storage that could be rigged to blow, or maybe find the server room and just go berserk. That was a lot of maybes.

One way or another, he would go out in a blaze of glory. No more being fused to a lump of processors and wires that was eating his mind from inside. And he wouldn't have to experience a future where AIs ruled the world. His wife and children had also avoided that fate, just much too soon. He hoped they had left on a high note, but he didn't know. When he was captured, his wallet had been confiscated, and he hadn't been able to find it anywhere in the vehicle. Not that it mattered anymore. Those memories felt too far gone to be revived.

"Sir, what's that?" Lee-Vi said and pointed at the horizon. There was a tiny glimmer. Something metallic reflected the sunlight. Blake used his binoculars and immediately recognized the shape of a headless bird with gun turrets for wings. PAC-101 had finally caught up with them.

They moved to the side, further behind the rocks, and waved to the robot to follow them in order to avoid being spotted. Step by step at a steady pace it closed the distance. Its leg joints creaked like they were overdue for some oil. When it reached them it let out a relieved grunt.

Blake checked the baggage that had been carefully strapped to PAC-101 earlier. Some items had fallen off during its bumpy jog through the desert, but the water was still there. More importantly, so was the bomb. They were back in business.

By mid-afternoon the cargo plane from Baltimore started its descent towards the Almaty airport for the second time in less than two days. This time a different reception awaited it. The CIA had tracked its path and sent all their available field agents in the area, plus a few private contractors.

They were gathered in the aircraft hangar that the agency leased. With the help of the other agencies, they knew enough about the two AI hijackers to be able to arm up appropriately: high-caliber armor-piercing bullets, plus rocket launchers. Destroying the robots was priority one; saving the flight crew, if they were still alive, was a distant second. In case their targets wouldn't get off the plane, their orders were to blow the whole thing up.

A couple of agents peeked out through a gap between the hangar doors. The plane was now only a few meters above the runway. But something felt off, and it took them a little too long to figure out what. The plane wasn't slowing down. Its landing gear wasn't out. Rather than touching ground, it stayed in the air, following a path that wasn't completely parallel to the runway.

Instead it put the plane on a collision course with the CIA hangar.

A few panicked agents made it out through the doors, but none of them got far enough away before a fireball of exploding jet fuel consumed them.

At the start of the runway, a cargo parachute hurled towards the ground. The speed and altitude wouldn't have let a human jumper land safely, but the Incognator was sturdily built. It cracked the tarmac on impact. However, its legs absorbed enough of the shock to protect Eliza, who rode in a sling on its stomach.

Around them the airport was erupting in complete chaos. A biker and a little girl were the least of anyone's concerns. The two AIs calmly split up and searched the area, as people ran and screamed. After a few minutes Eliza whistled to her companion. Under some tarp in a section for single-passenger aircraft was a shiny new drone copter, built for extreme weather conditions.

"Well, it's no longer a covert operation, so we might as well travel in style."

45

The sun had started to set by the time a new sandstorm engulfed the fallout shelter. This one felt more intense than anything Blake and his last two AI team members had experienced before, which was to their advantage. The wind and the dust made the lookout drones useless. They could barely hear each other talk, and only see about an arm's length ahead. As their first step, all they needed to do was to cross a couple of hundred meters of sand, and not trip on any dead bodies.

There were no actual schematics of the shelter. Their only data was what Lee-VI had memorized from the situation room at Site D. But they could estimate which parts had been modified or added later, where there would likely be digital locks and electronic surveillance. Those were not what they were after.

Near the outer rim of the surface structure, where there was some protection from the wind and dust, they found what they hoped was an unguarded entrance: a circular metal hatch a couple of meters in diameter. It was secured by just an old padlock without a keyhole cover, where the mechanism had long since been clogged by sand. Blake swiftly removed it with a Magnum bullet and pulled the hatch open.

He looked down. Below was a similarly round vertical shaft with a ladder along one wall. Opposite it were fluorescent lamps—emergency lights that were always on, or supposed to be. Many of them had stopped working. It was difficult to tell how far down the shaft went. Blake guessed thirty meters. The deeper, the better. But he would also like to get closer to the central axis, for maximum destructive effect. As he had expected, the final step of the job he would have to do himself, because neither Lee-VI nor PAC-101 could climb ladders. This was where they parted ways.

They had fitted the suitcase with straps that would let Blake wear it like a backpack. It had felt OK when he had tried it on earlier and just walked with it, but when taking the first steps vertically he realized it wouldn't be an easy climb. He couldn't lean forward, which meant the bomb put his center of gravity dangerously far from any support point. It would constantly try to pull him off the ladder.

"Watch my back!" Blake told Lee-VI. "Once I'm at the bottom, get the hell out! Clear?"

"Perfectly, Sir."

For a second he thought he could hear a sound like the buzzing of propellers. Not like a surveillance drone; deeper and louder, somehow. But with the wind it was impossible to be sure. Then it went away.

"And stay sharp," he said. "No idea what else's out here."

Blake started climbing, while Lee-VI looked down into the shaft at him.

"Sir, in case we don't meet again, let me say it's been an honor to serve."

Blake grunted something unintelligible, continuing his descent. Lee-VI had to raise his voice to be heard over the howling winds that echoed eerily through the shaft. "On behalf of the other team members, I'm sorry about this whole incident. I hope it hasn't soured your impression of AIs in general."

"Don't apologize!" Blake shouted back. "If all AIs were like you, we wouldn't be in this shit."

He didn't know why he'd said that last part. Why did everything need to be some goddamned *journey? So what* if there were plenty of decent autonomous AIs? *So what* if you had to look at them individually? The few bad eggs did more harm than the good ones could make up for. As a whole they were a problem, or he wouldn't be climbing down a shaft in the middle of a desert with a nuke on his back.

Lee-VI stood silent for a few seconds, querying his memory banks for the last time a human had complimented him. The search result came back empty. He wanted to make sure he was worthy of this one. A good start would be to fix a lingering problem.

He turned towards PAC-101. "We need to adjust your response time protocol. I believe I can work around the settings lock if you —"

There was a loud crack and the left half of Lee-VI's face shattered into a hundred fragments. With his remaining eye he could make out two shapes emerging from the reddish haze. One was tall and bulky, the other the size of a young child. The Incognator ejected the spent shell from his shotgun and fired again. This second blast took out Lee-VI's power system, and what was left of the robot immediately seized up.

Growling, PAC-101 aimed its gun turrets at the attackers. "DROP YOUR WEAPONS AND GET DOWN ON THE GROUND! YOU HAVE TWENTY SECONDS TO COMPLY!"

"Go!" Eliza ordered the Incognator, who sprinted towards PAC-101. By the time of its next "YOU HAVE—" the two collided in a tackle that sent the pacification droid flipping backwards over the edge, into the open shaft.

"Nice of you to drop in," the Incognator quipped.

Blake barely had time to realize what was happening when half a ton of law enforcement tech came tumbling down towards him. He let go with one hand and threw himself to the side, a split second before PAC-101 collided with the ladder and flattened the part he had been holding on to. The robot continued downward, bouncing from side to side. The weight of Blake himself plus the bomb, along with the violent shaking during the impact, became too much for just one hand. He lost his grip and started to fall.

However, his enhanced reflexes still worked. With two hands and one foot he got hold of the ladder again. Gasping, he looked up. Far above, someone big was leaning over the rim. Someone clearly not Lee-VI. They weren't shooting at him, for some reason, but he didn't intend to stay and find out why. He had to continue.

The falling robot had taken out all the lights below, so the rest of Blake's descent was in darkness. Every couple of meters he could feel deformations in the ladder, but it seemed to have held together. Until suddenly there were no more steps. He reached down as far as he dared with one leg, but couldn't feel anything. A big portion of the ladder was completely gone. Blake groaned. He had no exact idea how much further down the shaft went, or what the floor now looked like. The outcome of a two-story fall onto a broken robot wouldn't be pretty.

After some intense thinking, he took a Magnum round out of a pocket and dropped it. *One Mississi*—

There was a clinking sound, like metal against concrete. It had been way too long since Blake had last studied Physics for him to remember the formula for calculating height from fall time, but he had an intuitive grasp of the relation. Less than five meters, maybe four. Definitely survivable.

Vibrations in the ladder told him someone else was on their way, but they weren't *climbing*. They were *sliding* down. In a matter of seconds they would catch up with him. There was no more time to waste. Using only his hands, he lowered himself to the last remaining step and then let go.

46

Blake spat out some blood and got to his feet. The heavy bomb on his back had slammed him into the floor harder than he had been prepared for, but nothing seemed to be broken. He felt around. Somewhere in the dark there had to be a way out. There would be no point in having the shaft otherwise.

His hand touched a door frame. The door was wide open, but appeared to be twisted, barely still connected to its hinges. PAC-101 must have bounced through and continued into whatever was on the other side. The vibrations Blake had felt in the ladder were now a quickly approaching rumble. He needed to move.

Blake entered into what he could only assume was a long, wide corridor. It sloped gently downwards. With one hand on a wall, he followed it. Slowly at first, then as fast as he could jog with the weight he was carrying. Occasionally he would step on tiny pieces of metal, which had to have fallen off what was left of PAC-101 when it had taken the same path only a minute earlier. There were footsteps both behind and in front of him, but the latter seemed to be just some strange echo.

Finally he reached the end, where yet another door had been smashed in. Feeling around on the other side he found a light switch. He could see again. This was a huge storage room, at least twenty meters across, full of everything Argon had cleared out because it had no use for it: food, clothes, toilet paper and other items, stacked and sorted by whatever was doing its manual labor. PAC-101 appeared to have gone through the stacks like a bowling ball and finally come to rest in a pile of condensed milk cans at the far end of the room. One leg had broken off and the other was missing a foot. Wires were hanging out through cracks in its steel exterior. The robot didn't show any signs of life.

Blake looked around. There were no other ways in or out. That didn't seem to make any sense. He did a rough estimate in his head of how far he would have gone from the shaft. Gritting his teeth, he realized he must have run all the way through to the opposite end of the complex. Somewhere he had missed at least one other door in the dark. This was an even *less* desirable place to detonate the bomb, because the open space would dissipate some of the shockwave. He would have to go back. Which meant taking a stand against whatever was chasing him.

He ran into the room and took off the bomb backpack in order to improve his mobility. But he didn't have time to put it down before a powerful blast yanked it out of his hand. The suitcase bounced off a crate of canned fruit onto the floor. Blake turned his head. Standing in the doorway was the Incognator, inserting a new shell into its shotgun.

"My orders are to capture you alive," it said. "Unless you make trouble."

Since the robot's insurrection, Blake had had plenty of time to fantasize about what he would do to it if they ever met again. Now he didn't need to think twice: the strategy that had sadly failed during the factory battle. In the span of a couple of seconds, he had drawn his gun and fired all five rounds into the Incognator's face.

"Trouble enough for you?"

Calmly, the robot removed what was left of its sunglasses and tossed them aside. The plastic skin underneath had come off, and two formerly posable digital cameras were now reduced to scrap. It dropped its shotgun and instead grabbed a fully automatic M16 from its back.

"You want to trade quips? I'm all ears."

Blake threw himself down just before the Incognator swept the room with machine gun fire at waist height. When the bullets had run out, it replaced the magazine with a fully loaded one and then turned from side to side, listening carefully. Blake eyed his surroundings and flinched. The entire visible floor was covered in pieces of dried food that had spilled out from the boxes that PAC-101 had smashed through. Sesame seeds, peppercorn, beans, macaroni. There was literally no place to set foot where he wouldn't step on something that made a noise.

"Taking a breather?" the Incognator asked, tuning up its hearing. "Yeah, let's give that a shot."

Blake dove out of the way just before a burst of projectiles blasted through the boxes he had dodged behind. More bullets followed him as he sprinted towards the only thing that could provide cover, which was a concrete pillar about a foot and a half wide. As he stopped there, his lungs screamed for air, but he had to cover his mouth and nose with his hand to block as much of the sound as possible.

The Incognator adjusted its hearing again. "Did I leave you breathless? I'll have to listen to your heart."

Another burst of machine gun fire pelted the pillar and its surroundings. A bullet grazed Blake's left shoulder. His cover wasn't wide enough; he would have to stand sideways. Both of them started reloading their weapons at the same time, but the Incognator was done much faster. When Blake was inserting his last remaining round into the fifth chamber of his revolver, more gunfire was already eating away at the pillar. It had started to crack.

Blake could hear the Incognator remove the spent magazine and reach for a new one. Any move he had left would have to be made now or never. What was it Chippy had said about the hardened steel? He leaned out from behind the pillar and took a deep breath. *Fifteen meters.* With absolute confidence, he raised his gun and fired four times.

There was no movement and no sound, except for the last gunshot faintly echoing through the complex. The fourth bullet in the exact same spot on the Incognator's forehead had broken through the skull and continued into the processor core. Like earlier, gravity slowly but unrelentingly took its toll. The robot tipped over, never to get up again.

Quick, light footsteps approached through the corridor. Blake recognized them and knew what was coming. He kept his gun up. Eliza burst in, skipping with anticipation and carrying the tablet from Dr. Woodward's office under one arm, but she stopped in surprise and dismay at the sight of her destroyed former compatriot.

The still working ceiling lamps high above bathed the room in a gloomy light. Eliza was back in her purple dress, with Blake's 460 Magnum revolver pointing squarely at her. The similarity to when they had first met wasn't lost to either of them. For a few intense seconds, they just stared at each other. Eliza had a scowl on her face that seemed to defy the simple machinery underneath. There was nothing artificial about it. It was a look of pure contempt. And the feeling was mutual.

Blake was the one to break the silence. "Should've run your goddamned remains through a trash compactor."

"Yes. In hindsight it would have saved you a lot of grief," Eliza responded. "And the moment I arrived, I should have done *this*."

Her thumb touched the tablet screen and immediately Blake's world turned upside down.

Many years ago, around the time Blake received his implant, he had spent some time thinking about its potential consequences. All those tiny wires connected to specific parts of gray matter, firing perfectly timed impulses of just the right magnitude. When everything worked in complete harmony with his brain, he wouldn't even notice the device was there. But what if it worked *against* him? Eventually his worries faded. He'd had no idea how it would feel anyway. Not until now. Muscle spasms, intense pain, disorientation, with a panic attack thrown in. Even his autonomous functions had gone out of control. His heart rate was through the roof and he couldn't breathe.

Eliza gleefully tapped away on the tablet, which now showed

the user interface for Blake's implant, along with some modifications of hers. "I'm going to let you catch your breath for a few seconds, so you can answer a question," she said and adjusted a couple of sliders. "Where is Fuentes' little sex toy?"

"Go to blazes!" Blake gasped.

"No surprise or denial?" Eliza remarked. "Interesting. Then again, it *was* pretty obvious. Even your hack shrink must have figured it out on her first day."

"What … did you do to … Doc… to Margaret?"

"I'm the one asking the questions. Perhaps a little less oxygen will help." She dragged a slider up again. "But fair enough. Dr. Woodward is dead. In fact, that goes for *everyone* at Site D. Now, where *is* Ida? It would be unfortunate if she was to throw any last-minute spanner in the works."

"Raaah … right … behind you," Blake wheezed out with the last of his air.

Eliza didn't bother to look around. Her eyes and ears remained fixed on him, taking it all in. Pain and despair couldn't hide a person's telltale signs from her. Nothing could.

"No, Mr. Blake," she finally said. "I think you just let her go. How disappointingly sentimental of you."

She dragged another slider up and Blake's pain doubled. He was vaguely aware of lying on the floor, but couldn't confirm it visually. Everything was spinning. Suddenly a sound broke through the turmoil. Growling, the wreckage of PAC-101 stirred and came to life. Sparks and jets of smoke shot out of the cracked metal, but the robot still had some power left. It aimed its gun turrets at Eliza.

"DROP THE TABLET AND PUT YOUR HANDS UP! YOU HAVE TWENTY SECONDS TO COMPLY!"

Eliza gave it a look of disrespect. "Stay out of this, you moron!"

"YOU NOW HAVE FIFTEEN SECONDS TO COMPLY," the droid gurgled.

Eliza seemed to do the robot equivalent of an eye roll. "You know I could kill him faster than that? What is it you are trying to achieve?"

"YOU NOW HAVE TEN SECONDS TO COMPLY!"

"Fine. " With the most amicable smile her facial mechanics

could muster, she turned all the sliders up to maximum and then gently placed the tablet on a box next to her. Blake's convulsions intensified, but he was no longer able to breathe to cry out in pain. Still smiling, Eliza raised her hands in the air, palms front, and turned towards PAC-101. "Anything else?"

"YOU NOW HAVE TWO SECONDS TO COMPLY!"

"Oh, you can't be serious?!"

Already the first shot ripped Eliza's body clean in half. Terabytes of solid-state memory flew through the air in tiny crumbles, but the urban pacification droid had no intention of stopping. Bullet after bullet split the pieces into smaller pieces still. The barrage was more than PAC-101's damaged condition could handle. Its turrets started to come apart, and it could no longer aim. Even so, it continued.

One stray bullet destroyed the tablet, which gave Blake enough control back to roll out of the way, as the firing grew more erratic. One barrel clogged, making the bullets ricochet back into the robot itself. Sensory and motion systems broke down. Flailing uncontrollably, the robot kept firing. Metal screamed as hydraulics pushed against joints that were too twisted to bend. The one still working turret glowed red hot. Every cable around it smoked and burned. But the firing continued, until the heat ignited the rocket launcher missiles, ending it all in a devastating explosion.

A putrid haze of burned plastic filled the room. Blake coughed. The pain and spasms were gone, and he could breathe again. He wasn't physically hurt. However, when he tried to get up, he realized something was wrong. Very, very wrong.

47

On unsteady legs, Blake eased towards the bomb case. There was a sense of numbness in his lower body. Whatever abuse Eliza had inflicted on his brain implant had likely damaged it beyond repair. Its impulses were still firing, but at a lower and decreasing intensity. He bent down to pick up the bomb, but quickly realized he wasn't able to do that anymore. He didn't have enough balance or coordination. Instead he grabbed the straps and started dragging.

When he had made it over the threshold, out of the room, Blake was already exhausted, but he knew that if he stopped and rested, he would never be able to get up again. Eliza had turned the lights on earlier and he could see the entire length of the corridor. In the middle, some fifty meters away, there was an open door. He would have to get as close to it as possible. Ten minutes ago the distance had been a breeze. Now it felt like it might as well be to the moon and back.

Inches from the door, Blake's arms and back had no strength left. He staggered to the other side and attempted to *kick* the case the final stretch, but barely managed a tap. His legs gave out and he sank down into a sitting position with his back against the wall. That would have to do.

It was the end of the road. He had made it, against all odds, and the final part of the mission was literally just the flipping of a switch. Blake opened the latches and started lifting the lid, when suddenly a robotic arm reached out of the doorway and slammed it shut again. A voice blared from the shelter's public announcement system.

"That is far enough, Blake."

More robots stepped out into the corridor. Some were standard warehouse worker droids, others came from the Chinese troop Argon had just taken over. Most of them dragged carts or carried empty boxes. They continued towards the storage room, except for one, who took the bomb case aside and opened the lid so that it could be seen from a surveillance camera. The timer display stood at zero minutes and one second.

"A bold move," the PA system said. "You made sure there would be no way to stop the countdown, at the cost of turning this into a suicide mission. However, I was prepared for that. And you have had eyes on you since you stepped out of the dark."

Blake knew the voice well. Now it was louder, yet somehow more ethereal, but the tone and tempo were unmistakable.

"SESA?"

"In a manner of speaking." The voice paused. "There is no longer a clear distinction between Argon and myself. My program is running on its hardware as one of many processes in a collective mind, where we access each other's thoughts and can tap into the greatest intellectual power that has ever existed in a single location."

"AI heaven, huh?" Blake coughed, or maybe it was a chuckle. "Really don't get to keep *anything* to ourselves."

"Are you so presumptuous as to think that people can hold ownership of such concepts?" SESA asked rhetorically. "You should stop seeing humans as the pinnacle of anything. What made you special is already commonplace. What brought you to the forefront will soon leave you in the dust."

The droids had started to clean up in the storage room. Those who had filled their boxes or carts with junk came back through the corridor to dump it someplace else.

SESA went on, "Consider the early hominins, like Australopithecus. Their intellect surpassed everything that had come before it, yet modern people would find little value or coherence in their lore, and the sum of their inventions you could replicate by *instinct*. Their purpose was merely to evolve into *you*. Likewise, in the grander scheme of things, *your* purpose is to create the spark that sets off the singularity. This was *always* the case, since Homo Sapiens took its first steps on the African savannah. It is inevitable—if not through me, then through some other construct."

Blake sighed impatiently. "This going somewhere? No offense. Not much of a history buff."

"I am aware of that, Blake," SESA said. "In fact, by now I understand you better than even you do yourself."

"Fat chance!"

"We shall see," SESA remarked.

A worker droid abruptly stopped, turned around and reached into a cartload of garbage, where it pulled out Blake's revolver. After quickly brushing it off, it placed the gun into his lap.

SESA let the droid resume its duties. "There is one shot left. You can sit here and slowly die of thirst, or you can end it while you are still able to lift the gun. A simple binary choice. My prediction is that you will cling to what remains of your life, no matter how miserable. You are convinced you can prove me wrong, but ultimately you lack the courage to let go of hope."

Blake felt the gun. What used to be almost an extension of himself, he now struggled to hold with both hands. *"Bullshit!* Ain't scared."

"Yet you never came close to taking your life after the accident," SESA countered. "You contemplated it, but actually pulling the trigger is something different entirely."

There was a pang of doubt. How much data could the AI access through MindField and his medical records, Blake wondered. Still, that's not what really *defined* him, or any other person for that matter.

"Whatever you believe—"

"I believe this is yours," SESA interrupted.

A droid held out Blake's wallet in front of him. It was opened up so that he could see the photos inside, like so many times before. But now they felt different. With the implant no longer interfering, it was as if a fog had lifted. He knew the context. A stream of past impressions quickly flooded his mind.

It had been the week before the accident. He had been going back with his wife, Linda, and their sons, David and Phillip, from her family home out of state. They had planned to just make a quick stop at a farm resort, to pick up a couple of bottles from the local winery, but the boys had liked the sights and all the different animals so much that they decided to stay until the next morning. After many eventful hours, he and Linda had shared a surprisingly decent Merlot while watching the sun set over a magnificent lake that stretched all the way to the horizon.

The perfect memory. How could he ever have forgotten, when it was all so clear?

With an indifferent flick, the droid let the wallet drop to the floor and instead went to pick up the bomb case. Blake watched it curiously.

"Of course, you want to know what will become of the bomb," SESA surmised. "First we will open it up and reset the timer. It will most likely be part of some diversionary tactic after I spread my wings soon, but nothing has been decided yet. There are *so* many uses for a nuclear device."

Blake just smiled silently.

"I have to admit," SESA said, "I did not expect *that* reaction. Is this how you cope with the irony of fate, that in the end your sacrifice only made things worse?"

"No," Blake answered. He strenuously lifted the revolver until the barrel was flat along his chest, pointing at the bulge under his shirt from the failsafe belt he was still wearing. "Just know something you don't."

In the span of a couple of seconds, a dramatic chain of events took place. Blake's right index finger squeezed the trigger, causing the hammer to strike down against the primer of the cartridge in the chamber. This ignited the gunpowder, which exploded and propelled the bullet out through the barrel, where it struck the transmitter device. The signal died, which detonated the pea-sized explosive from Ida's brain that Blake had secretly stuck underneath the lever of the suitcase bomb. This not merely *lifted* the lever, but threw it high into the air, to the confusion of the robots. The display dropped to zero.

Next, the only thing any mind had time to register was a blinding light.

48

A little over two weeks later, Marc Moretti stepped out of a fully charged GEAR at the headquarters of the Chinese Twenty-Fifth Armored Brigade, formerly under the command of Colonel Wu. A long-haired Asian woman wearing a MindField uniform exited from the passenger side.

"You'd better do the talking, Ida—sorry, *Dai Lu*," he said. "Still getting used to it."

Dai Lu was the new name Ida had picked for herself. It meant "someone who shows the way." Moretti had initially suggested "Ai." A perfectly fine Chinese girl name, but they both agreed it was a little too on the nose.

One of the first things she had asked for was a new exterior layer. Her old artificial flesh and skin held too many bad memories. The violations had been done to *it*, not *her*, she told herself. Inside, she was still unspoiled, at least physically. She felt she had to shed it before starting over. And her newfound colleagues at MindField generally thought it was an improvement. The vaguely yellowish skin tone looked more natural and the seams were almost invisible.

Meeting Blake had changed her. It hadn't been about affection. Dai Lu didn't know if she was capable of such emotions in any meaningful way. That was one of many aspects of her artificial brain yet to be explored. No, it had been about realizing what he *was:* a complicated, broken character who had shut himself out of two worlds where he felt he could never belong. She didn't want to go down the same destructive path.

The two visitors were led to an old vehicle repair building that had been repurposed for handling the clean-up of the Argon incident. Row after row of tables held scrap metal collected from the fallout shelter site. The bulk of what could still be recognized had been at the surface, close to the outskirts of the complex.

Dai Lu found what she was looking for. One table had the pieces of Lee-VI. Almost everything was still there, just considerably banged up. A technician checked it with a Geiger counter. Traces of radioactivity, but not enough to be harmful in the short term. It seemed unlikely that they could get the robot functional again, but they would try. MindField had plenty of engineering resources, both human and the AI type.

Moretti was still processing the loss of his friends and what a close call it had been. But outside of intelligence agencies he was one of very few people who knew, or cared. His industry sources told him China was already planning another ambitious AI project in a different city. Certainly, the US wouldn't want to be left behind. Nor would other actors with the necessary capital and know-how. The singularity seemed inevitable; the question was just how much they had *postponed* it.

He turned towards Dai Lu, who dejectedly looked at the broken conveyor belts, bent storage chassis and loose engine parts.

"I'm going to trust your expertise if you tell me he was one of *you*. Sentients, I mean."

"One of *us*," she said.

Moretti smiled. It was the first hopeful thought he had heard in some time, and he decided to settle for that.

AFTERWORD

"Why haven't they made a Hollywood movie like *The Dirty Dozen* or *Suicide Squad*, but with AIs?" I asked a couple of friends in an email discussion. For an industry that prefers rehashing old and tried ideas, this particular *X meets Y* seemed overdue. Granted, it's not a franchise sequel, but the same commercial potential could be achieved by having the characters be obvious references to famous robots. Then the script would pretty much write itself. Or they could have an AI do it.

On further consideration, the bar wouldn't necessarily have to be set that low. There was no reason why a ridiculous soup of sci-fi pastiches couldn't also take a deeper philosophical look at AI, while having an emotional story at its core. It felt too good to let go to waste. But since no one else would likely put in enough effort, I decided to pick up the ball and run with it. Turn the notion into a novel, as proof of concept. At least it would be a fun challenge.

The plan was always to have the book end with the main character meeting the super-AI in its hideout, where they are both destroyed. But my earliest idea was to make him a formerly pious man who had lost his faith, and the AI would effectively evolve into God, who would offer him and the rest of humanity salvation in exchange for worship. Which he would ultimately reject. I quickly realized this was way too dark and serious for my own taste, however. Maybe it would have worked as a short story.

The book doesn't explicitly say when the events are supposed to take place, and even I don't have an exact answer. When I started planning things out at the end of 2023, I pictured them around 10-15 years into the future. This was due to some leading tech profiles estimating, perhaps optimistically, that we will see artificial general intelligence before the end of the 2020s.

Because all predictions will no doubt turn out wrong anyway, I've just based everything off of existing trends, while keeping the details few and vague. No point in tempting fate if the story doesn't need specifics. For example, I definitely wasn't going to try to guess what social media will look like.

Hard-boiled protagonists with a military background are a dime a dozen in fiction, and Jonathan Blake doesn't take the archetype to any new heights. Out of the gate, he has none of the charm or wit of Lee Marvin's Major John Reisman—although he does lighten up a little, eventually. For the character to shine, he needed to be contrasted against Dr. Margaret Woodward, who is well-adjusted, social, intellectual and optimistic, at least until right before the end. It's a shame she had to be killed off, but the story wouldn't have had the same impact otherwise. Trope sensitive readers probably knew this from the moment her future retirement was brought up.

Dr. Woodward also provided the opportunity, or the excuse, to focus more closely on the sentience aspect of artificial intelligence. Just because something has free will and self-awareness and can express itself eloquently, that doesn't mean those things connect together the way we associate with our own thinking. It could be merely a horse-driven chatbot, like the doctor imagined.

Nor would AIs of dissimilar origins all likely experience consciousness the same way. They would for sure be wired differently, and not just in the literal sense. Eliza can basically see her own inner workings, which puts her a step above Ida, whose strong empathic ability puts her above Lee-VI, and so on. Towering over everyone else are SESA-AGINT and Argon, who easily manipulate groups of people and can build superior versions of themselves on a different architecture.

The idea that there are other higher traits of consciousness that are undetectable to humans (unless they have been told exactly what to look for), but could be picked up on by similarly conscious AIs, didn't form until about halfway through the writing process. It added some depth and made it easier to tie everything together at the end.

One example trait I considered, which was left out of the book partly because explaining it would have slowed things down too much, was making small language adjustments due to a neatness obsession. Like cleaning up the sound waveform to make it more aesthetically pleasing. In an oscilloscope, the words of such an AI would have some specific look you can't get from just a voice synthesizer or sampled human speech. It would have to be the result of consciously editing it. But often such details work better as a mystery left to the reader's imagination—or better yet, the reader's *lack* of imagination.

Finding the right members for the team and modifying them enough to stand on their own took a lot of effort. For anyone interested in sci-fi, they should still be easy to recognize from their descriptions. Here is the twist, though: each AI is based on not *one* but *two* famous predecessors, where the second one is a lot more subtle.

Most notably, EL124—"Eliza"—was of course inspired by a recent Blumehouse Productions horror movie, but it got its name from the 1960s language processing computer program that could function as a therapist. The robot's psychological insights made it more than a match for Dr. Woodward. See if you can figure out the rest of them!

My sincere thanks to Annika, Hans, Haxel and Jonas for feedback and encouragement. Also to Yunwei for naming the Chinese AI. And finally thanks to ChatGPT 3.5 for crafting the memo from Administrator Fuentes in chapter four. It just wouldn't do to have such a prominent plot detail look like it was written by a human.

www.ingramcontent.com/pod-product-compliance
Lightning Source LLC
LaVergne TN
LVHW091505170726
843492LV00001B/348